Sirshendu Mukherjee was born on 2nd November 1935 at Maimansingh, now in Bangladesh. After doing his Intermediate in Arts from the Victoria College in Coochbehar, he graduated from the Calcutta University.

Sirshendu Mukherjee began his career as a schoolteacher and is presently attached to the *Ananda Bazar Patrika*, Kolkata. His first novel, *Ghoonpoka* (The Woodworm) was published in 1967. Since then, he has written a number of novels and innumerable short stories. *Ujan, Parapar, Jao Pakhi, Manab Jamin* and *Parthiba* are some of his outstanding works. Sirshendu is considered one of the finest writers of Bangla literary fiction today.

His honours include the Sahitya Akademi Award for *Manab Jamin* in 1989 and the Vidyasagar Prize for his contribution to children's literature in 1985. He has also been awarded the prestigious Ananda Purashkar twice.

Santanu Sinha Chaudhuri was born in Calcutta in 1951. He studied in Ballygunge Government High School, Calcutta and Visva-Bharati University in Santiniketan, West Bengal. Starting his career in a factory in rural West Bengal, he then worked as a banker for twenty-four years.

Translating works of Bangla literary fiction into English is more than a serious hobby for him. His published translations include an anthology of Dibyendu Palit's short stories – *The Faces and Other Stories* and Bibhuti Bhushan Bandopadhyay's unforgettable novella for children – *The Mountain of the Moon*. He has also translated Sirshendu Mukherjee's *Manab Jamin* (Of Men and Earth). Readers are welcome to contact him at santanusc@yahoo.com.

Tomorrow, I Promise ...

Stories by

Sirshendu Mukherjee

Translated by

Santanu Sinha Chaudhuri

ALCHEMY

First published in 2005 by

ALCHEMY™

an imprint of

Mehras

15, Bankim Chatterjee Street
2nd Floor, Kolkata-700 073

4767/23, Pratap Street Darya Ganj,
New Delhi-110 002

G-1 & 2, Ghaswalla Towers,
PG Solanki Path, Off Lamington Road
Mumbai-400 007

Cover Design: Ajoy Gupta

Printed in India by Shivam Sundaram at Tara Offset, New Delhi

ISBN No. 81-8046-026-6

2 4 6 8 10 9 7 5 3 1

Contents

Foreword

When we pick up a book for the first time, certain expectations build up in our mind. I am sure, as you read these lines, you too would look forward to something from this slender volume. You would possibly want to spend a pleasant day with this book on a train, or by the sea. Or perhaps, you would expect these pages to unravel some of the mysteries that lie beneath the surface of human beings, or the subtle nuances of their relationships. Or, do you look forward to a book that has to be preserved in your bookshelf, so that you might pick it up again, maybe years later, on a rainy day or in a frosty evening?

Sirshendu Mukherjee is a rare author who fulfils all these expectations, and more. A writer of lyrical prose, he is brilliantly witty and a pleasure to read. And his works offer much more than just the pleasure of reading. He often deals with elemental issues that shape our lives and keep us guessing at the crossroads. But he does so without adopting a sombre style. Consequently, he is both critically acclaimed and immensely popular among the readers of Bangla literary fiction.

Sirshendu's characters are ordinary people; many of them live next door, or in a small bungalow across the road. But more interestingly, he often writes about the wretched of the earth, the people who have been marginalised by the relentless march of history and civilisation: a castaway who dreams of becoming a great thief someday; the little son of a blind beggar marooned in a sea of lovelessness and insecurity; an illegitimate offspring of a rich landlord; a petty conman who genuinely wants to reform himself; a plain Jane prostitute who struggles to secure custom; the village lunatic who doubles up as a fake sadhu .... The list is endless. What is fascinating about Sirshendu Mukherjee is not the wide range of his characters alone, but the clear strokes with which he paints the landscapes of their minds. This has been possible because Sirshendu loves to be with people; he detests solitude. He visits remote villages and stays with ordinary people, sharing thoughts and food with them. And when we see our familiar society through the eyes of these dispossessed people, we come face to face with the sidereal injustices that rule this world, the devious rules of an unfair game that marginalise countless humans who love life as much as you and I do. But at the end of the day, Sirshendu's stories are not about deprivation and defeat, they are about hope and the indomitable spirit of man.

The author believes that a positive force governs our life; every living being wants to be alive, death is a dreadful refuge. In an interview, he tells me that he does not end his stories with a mournful sigh, he takes pains to end them on a positive note. To do the contrary would be easier; the most facile thing for an author is to kill one of his characters to terminate a story. On the other hand, the discernible reader would not accept a happy ending forced upon a storyline! Therefore Sirshendu travels circuitous paths to make endings both happy and credible. Some readers have told him that they rediscovered their desire to live after reading his works. And that, the author feels, is his greatest reward.

Sirshendu Mukherjee's characters are not black and white ones, they display the many in-between shades of grey, usually missed by an ordinary observer. And like all fine authors, he has a knack of looking at things from an unusual viewpoint. Often, he makes conventional wisdom stand on its head. He is sympathetic towards thieves and conmen without any visible signs of discomfort. His ghosts – he has written some unforgettable ghost stories – are not scary, they are good souls and always pleasant to deal with. In the story 'The Newspaper,' the author's sympathies are with a woman who does not conform to the accepted social mores, but in the end, he goes to the root of her tragedy, and offers us the delight of looking at her from the depth of her soul. Similarly, in the story 'I, I Alone …', Sirshendu looks at things through the eyes of an arrogant intruder, a failed terrorist and individual, who is unrepentant about his follies.

Sirshendu was born in a village on the banks of one of the mighty rivers of the world – the Brahmaputra. As a child, he was fascinated by the river that flowed along human relationships towards eternity. He says he has never outgrown the Brahmaputra. He has remained rooted to its soft saffron alluvial soil, like which, he too is patient and non-combative. Besides the Brahmaputra, his mother and grandfather shaped his mind. The river and these two individuals find a place in his writing again and again. Sirshendu feels his childhood has crossed its boundaries and continues to linger with him. As time scrapes off mysteries, as abrasive experiences and the heat and dust of life wear him out, the sound of a flowing river, the ethereal trill of a cuckoo and the fragrance of flowers waft in from his magical childhood. As he opens the window to his early days and looks back, he wants to live a thousand lives.

Sirshendu's father was in the railways and during his childhood, the family moved frequently to the hills, forests and teagardens of North Bengal, and many places in East Bengal and Bihar. As a grown up person too, he travelled widely. He has lived in cities like Coochbehar, Howrah and Calcutta and in fairytale small towns with arcane names like Domahani, Pandu, Lumding. Sirshendu Mukherjee is at his finest when he writes about these small places and their quiet, laid-back people. 'Tales from a Marketplace' is an illustration of his understanding of this milieu and his mastery over their language. His works encompass villages, small towns and the complexities of urban life, as would be seen from this anthology. Despite the wide variety of characters and social milieus about whom Sirshendu writes, there is a common thread that binds the entire body of his works. And the strands of that thread, in the author's own words, are the questions that have engaged human minds at all times: Who am I? What are *my* relationships with this infinite universe and the unending passage of time? These questions have been agitating, disturbing and driving Sirshendu Mukherjee since his childhood. He is also intrigued by the firmly shut doors at the two ends of human life – the unknowable world prior to birth and subsequent to death. And he occasionally dares to peep into this world, like he has done in 'The Storm.'

As a person, Sirshendu Mukherjee is unpretentious and modest. He credits his spiritual teacher, Thakur Anukul Chandra, for whatever he has achieved as a writer and individual. Since his childhood, Sirshendu suffered from recurring spells of melancholia. In his college days, he played table tennis, cricket and football with a fanatical enthusiasm, and spent little time with textbooks. He became the college table tennis champion in the first year itself. In a later writing, he explains that his involvement in sports was a defence mechanism against loneliness, fear of bizarre thoughts and his obsession with death. A happy spin-off of his sporting career is that games and sports are a recurring theme in his writing. In the crowd of serious thinkers in Bangla literature, Sirshendu brings in a whiff of fresh air with his often-hilarious sporting anecdotes. But that is a different issue. Sirshendu's past obsession with death is perhaps best exemplified in 'Death in a Dream'. Sirshendu says this is the most significant piece he has ever written. It took him one year and nine months and over two hundred sheets of foolscap paper to write these few pages. During that period, he could not write anything else either, and was devastated by self-doubt; his literary career nearly came to an end. At the age of thirty, he went through the last bout of anxiety syndrome. He writes:

> I suddenly realised that the long forgotten disease of melancholia, that bizarre feeling crept upon my body and mind like an attack of influenza.

> Terror stricken, I listened to the alarm bells that were reverberating through my existence. I became alone. I asked myself again and again – Why is the universe infinite? Why death? What is the purpose of life? And everything else? These questions kept injecting pitiless venom into my mind. My silent voice rent the air, 'Save me, save me!' I kept looking for a refuge in the waves of my consciousness … went on reading religious texts … someone was pushing me from the brink into an abyss of despondency. Days rolled on. I was on the verge of death.

At that hour of crisis, weighed down by uncertainty, doubt and disbelief, he went to meet his future mentor. Thakur Anukul Chandra saved him from imminent destruction and helped him overcome the crisis. It was a fortunate turnabout not only in Sirshendu Mukherjee's personal life, but also for Bangla literature.

This foreword is largely based on autobiographical writings of Sirshendu Mukherjee like *Ujan* (Upstream) and *Amar Ektu Kkhani Benche Thaka* (My Bits and Pieces Existence). It is also based on an interview I had with him in October 2004. The two hours that I spent with him on that autumn morning of crystal sun and cirrus clouds helped me understand his works better. I have stitched together his views on his own works with my understanding of them – which I know, is partial at best – and do hope this piece will offer the readers a glimpse into his literary life and his perspectives as an author. I am indeed grateful to Sirshendu Mukherjee for his support throughout this project.

My friends George Thomas, Damodar Menon, Uma Sankar and Basu Bimochan Bhattacharya have gone through most of the translated stories. They suggested some changes and have been generous with their encouragement. My wife Arundhati Sinha and daughter Sohini Sinha, though less charitable, have been great inspiration too.

Finally, I would like to express my deepest gratitude to the editor of this volume, Gita Rajan. She has saved me from many printed embarrassments and made my translations more readable.

Hyderabad — Santanu Sinha Chaudhuri
14 November 2004

Tales from a Market Place

Another day comes to an end behind Raja Fakirchand's hillock. A little while ago, a lonely shireesh tree had spread a quarter-mile long shadow; a much larger shadow, of a bird called night, swallowed it up quickly. Somewhere in the hillock are buried Fakirchand's seven pots of gold and heaps of gems and jewels, and indeed, his palace. Behind the hillock runs the railway line, and in

Raja Fakirchand: Fakir means pauper and Chand is a common suffix used in Bengali names. Here is a king named Fakir – Translator.

front, the gravelled road, with lots of trees and shadowy shrubs lining it on either side. Now, under a blanket of mist, the introspective winter evening looks a little gloomy. From somewhere on the road comes the sibilant sound of slippers being dragged on gravel. It's a pair of rubber slippers that has been repaired seven times. Yet, Nodiakumar hasn't cast them away.

In the confusion created by shadows, one can't be sure if it is Nodiakumar or his wife. Bheluram is partially blind because of cataract. His grandson, Khelaram, has gone to Beerpara to collect dues. As he hadn't come back, Bhelu went to the crossroads to check. He's returning now. A bus arrived from Beerpara and left. The boy wasn't in it. Bheluram makes a lot of fuss over his grandson. He feels he should have waited a little longer. But he can hardly afford to be away from his shop for long. His son Shobharam has turned into a thief, a rogue. A bloody scoundrel! Always high on hooch, he visits bad women. Shobharam's wife ran away. Later, Bhelu threw his son out, but has brought up his grandson with tender care. Shobharam, a real crook, doesn't care a fig for anyone except Bhelu. Whenever he is short on cash, he heads for his father's shop and tries to grab whatever he can lay his hands on. That is the reason Bhelu has been hurrying. He stops on hearing the noise made by the rubber slippers.

Is it Nodia or is it his wife? The problem is that these days Nodia's wife wears a dhoti, exactly the way a man does. She wears a shirt too, and has clipped off her long hair. No one can make out that she is a woman. She wears no bangles, nor does she put sindoor on the parting on her hair. She goes around the place even late into the night with impunity. She thinks she is a man and a devotee of goddess Kali. And she goes into a trance whenever goddess Kali decides to speak through her. Not only Bhelu, but everyone in and around the marketplace is scared of her, including Nodia.

Bhelu's eyes smart even in the worn-out evening light. Shading them with his right hand, he tries to figure out who it is. And asks cautiously, 'Who goes? Nodia?'

'Yes.' Nodia replies.

'Which way?'

'To the market.'

'Let's go together.'

'Yes, of course.'

The two walk side by side. Bheluram's tough leather shoes sound metallic on the road, Nodia's slippers make a gasping noise. This Nodia is an unhappy soul. If a man's wife turns man-like, then that man has a basketful of worries. But if anyone tries to gauge the reasons for Nodia's sorrow by looking at his slippers stitched at seven places, it would be a mistake. The state of the slippers is misleading. Two hefty workers slog away through the day in Nodia's 'Sri Sri Satyanarayana Sweet Shop'. One could say it is the only sweetmeat shop in the marketplace. Although a few more have cropped up recently with the sole intention of making Nodia a pauper, it is Nodia who has the lion's share of the business. The only downside is that he is a bit of a skinflint. He wouldn't buy shirts or shoes; when he goes out, scared of spending, he wouldn't carry any cash on his person. He would repair his slippers for the umpteenth time. Perhaps his wife had good reasons for turning into a male!

But then, every man has his share of misfortune. Nodia starts cribbing, 'On the next new moon, there will be a great feast in my house. Do you understand? My wife will sacrifice a goat with her own hands. Have you ever heard of a female slaughtering animals?'

Bheluram's family had migrated from the West three generations ago. He has become an authentic Bengali. But occasionally, he adulterates his otherwise perfect Bangla with a smattering of Hindi, just to keep in touch. He now says, in his hybrid lingo, 'Bhai Nodia, why do you still consider her as your aurat? She has turned into a male. Socho mat.'

'Little wonder you should talk like that. I'm drowning in sorrow and you people enjoy the fun for free!'

Bheluram makes appropriate noises with his shoes to underline his manliness and says, 'To keep such a woman on the straight and narrow, a man has to spank her thrice with his shoes.'

Saying this, he stops, lifts a foot and pointing at his naagra, says, 'And for that, one needs shoes like these! But what can you do? You don't even own a decent pair of shoes! Can you beat your wife with rubber slippers that flap like dog's ears?'

'Oh! Shut up!' Nodia retorts angrily, 'When Shobharam's mother chased you with a nora, you turned tail. Didn't you, you old bandicoot?'

Bheluram laughs heartily. His wife is no more. But he is immensely pleased to recall the happy moments when she used to chase him with a grinding stone. His eyes almost turn moist.

Shobharam slinks around the marketplace like a cat on the prowl. Things were different when his mother, Gandheswari, was alive. Even in those days, his father used to beat him with door latches and wooden slippers, but he wouldn't dare throw him out. Each and everyone, not excluding the ghosts living in the area, was scared of Shobharam's mother, Gandheswari. Bhelu couldn't have been an exception. She would haughtily ignore the police inspector or the Pathan moneylender. Compared to such distinguished persona, Bhelu was, at best, a cockroach. And the same Gandheswari protected Shobharam. Those days, Shobharam used to sing to himself: 'It's time for looting. Oh! What a wonderful feeling!' And how right was he. He stole to his heart's content from his father's wholesale trade of spices, jute, tobacco leaves, oilseeds and other merchandise. He had befriended spoilt brats and started smoking bidi at a very young age. When he was in class three, his academic career came to an abrupt end. Ma Gandheswari took him away from school as the teachers used to thrash him. For some time, he tried his hand at being an apprentice in his father's business. But it was not his cup of tea. And his father didn't make things easy either. Bhelu would create a scene over a few paise. Shobharam didn't care much for such piffle. When his wife came of age, his mother brought her over from her parent's place. But she was no match for him. By then, Shobharam, along with his friends, had tasted plenty of women. He found his rustic wife rather bland. Besides, she was cantankerous. Not that Shobharam minded. But she had her likes and dislikes too! Shobharam had got addicted to cannabis long ago. As also to liquor. The woman nagged him no end. After Khelaram's birth, she read him the riot act. But he was Gandheswari's protégé. One day, she beat the daylights out of her daughter-in-law with the pestle of a mortar used for husking paddy. Shobharam watched the thrashing with great admiration. He then prostrated before his mother to lick the dust off her feet. Six months later, his wife ran away leaving behind one-year-old Khelaram. Shobharam's father was always against him. His father bided his time till Gandheswari's death. Granting him his wish, Gandheswari died last year, leaving Shobharam alone and absolutely unprotected in this cruel heartless world. Bheluram kicked up a huge row immediately after Gandheswari's sraddha. Shobharam did try to protest, but Bhelu went to the extent of lodging a complaint against his own son with the Sub-Divisional Officer in the town. Shobharam left home in disgust.

But that hardly ended his difficulties. Lodging is not a problem. Shobharam is a nearly welcome guest in Jagan's shack at the Tirpai slum. But that doesn't mean he can live without money. One cannot depend on charity alone for things like booze. He has no work, no income and stealing isn't easy either. He had gone to the sub-divisional town and tried out some jobs. But that didn't work. He was hired as a domestic in a couple of households, but true to his instincts, he stole a few things, got caught, was beaten up and thrown out. His name figures in the police records. His life is in a shambles. He wanted to become a professional thief, but being a drug addict, he isn't in great shape. His hands tremble, his heart pounds and his head gets muddled very often. After observing thief Madna from close quarters, he has realised that it is not an easy profession. To become a good thief, one has to have self-control, confidence and intelligence; one has to make sacrifices. Madna exercises every morning, eats gram like a horse and drinks with restraint. Besides, he knows many mantras: mantras to keep evil spirits at bay, to keep a dog's muzzle shut, to ensure that people don't wake up ... It's not for no reason that Madna is a renowned thief today. If you wish to excel in any field, you need some qualities. Shobharam has none.

Therefore, occasionally, he is compelled to strike at Bheluram's store. His pleadings don't work anymore, nor do his threats. Bheluram has sized him up. Khelaram too shooes away his father. He has a pet dog, a pedigreed one; he often sets it after Shobharam. But even then, they are the only ones who disdainfully throw a few rupees at him. As Shobharam picks up the humiliating currency notes, tears well up in his eyes. His father, his very own son, the money legally his, and yet he has to beg!

This evening too, Shobharam has been furtively moving around the store trying to make out which way the wind is blowing. Bhelu's store and godown are in a lonely corner of the marketplace, where the air is heavy with a heady smell of spices. Khelaram's dog spots him from the first floor wooden balcony and barks fiercely. Shobharam looks up. A deadly animal. He mutters, 'Son of a bitch!'

Neither Bhelu nor Khela is in the shop. Only an old accountant is adding a long column of figures in a red clothbound accounting book. A few customers are waiting for Bhelu. And Khelaram's teacher Sreepati Karmakar has been sitting absently. Sreepati is a pleasant chap. He seems to be absorbed in thought at all hours. It is generally believed that he is by far the most highly educated person around. At the same time, Sreepati is a living testimony that one doesn't achieve much through education alone. He teaches in the primary school for a salary not worth mentioning. He also tutors an absolutely thick-headed Khelaram – grandson of the uneducated Bheluram and son of the half-wit Shobharam – two hours every evening to earn, maybe, fifty rupees a month. And during those two hours, Bheluram just sits behind his desk and makes at least one hundred rupees everyday.

Shobharam ventures into the store saying 'Ram Ram, Masterji!' with the air of an owner; as if it was a routine visit. The accountant looks at him, his brow furrowed. The cash box is at hand, but Shobharam knows it would be locked and there would be little inside. The bulk of the cash would be rolled up in a pouch and stuck in the waistline of Bheluram's dhoti.

Sreepati, the teacher, being absentminded by nature, doesn't recognise Shobharam. Sreepati is in a crumpled shirt and a dirty dhoti and his shock of hair is uncombed. With a faraway look, he asks, 'Aap kaun hain ji?'

Sreepati speaks chaste Hindi. On the first day he came to tutor Khelaram, he embarrassed Bheluram with his flowery Hindi garnished with Urdu expressions. Bhelu couldn't understand a word of what he said. After being in Bengal for three generations and after doing business with Bengalis, he knows little of Hindi. Once upon a time his family did live in the Hindi heartland. His wife could manage a bit of Hindi, but his grandson gets to learn the language only at school.

Hearing Sreepati's Hindi, Shobharam was unnerved. 'I am Khelaram's father, Masterji! Have you have forgotten?'

'Oh!' says Sreepati and sits motionless, wearing a melancholic look. His life has become hollow since he came to this small market town. Even his Hindi has become rusty as he has no one to talk to, not to mention the other subjects he had once studied. That stupid Khelaram cannot distinguish between left and right. During the two hours Sreepati is here, his student leaves him at least ten times to attend to customers. Khela has reached the ninth class after stumbling at every hurdle once or twice. He is unlikely to cross the steep ascent that now lies ahead of him. Yet, his grandfather Bheluram is keen that he passes B.Com. and masters the accounts. So Sreepati needles Khelaram occasionally, 'Can one become a B. Com. without brains?'

Shobharam asks most politely, 'You are alone Ji, where has Khela gone?'

Sreepati makes a sour face, 'How do I know? I am told he has gone to Beerpara or somewhere to collect dues. My time is up to eight. I'll leave after that.'

'Of course! Of course!' Shobharam shows his fatherly concern. 'How's Khela doing in studies, Masterji?'

'Nothing much can be done with him.'

The response pleases Shobharam. He says, 'I agree. I say, we are wasting money on him for nothing.'

As he talks, Shobharam sizes up the situation. There is nothing within reach that can be nipped. So he drums a beat on the cash box. At forty-five, he is no greenhorn. Khela too would be around twenty, twenty-two. Until last year, Shobharam lived in this store-cum-house. He was born under the supervision of midwife Bindi in the first floor of this shop. He grew up on the dusty roads of the marketplace. There is a courtyard behind, in which ma used to dry her pickles and papads. But he is now an outsider to these premises. Who could ever imagine that a father could become so distant?

Darkness descends over the marketplace. The labourers in the brick kiln can be heard singing. Some people have come to buy river fish from the stalls that open in the evening. They are haggling noisily. Otherwise, the marketplace is quiet. Winter has just arrived. From the look of it, it would be a severe one this year. Shobharam tightens the cotton wrap around himself. He doesn't believe in keeping the cold away with such external aids. There is nothing like hooch to fight the cold. Otherwise, one could get stoned on grass – and the cold would run away like those scuttling cats hit by his ma Gandheswari's firewood.

Shobharam can recognise his father's footfalls half a mile away. He gets up as soon as he hears them, looks around helplessly with groggy eyes: there's nothing to be pinched. A trader from Patharpota, who has come to buy locally made soap, is snoozing. His shoes are lying in front of the bench. A nice pair – absolutely new – it would cost at least thirty rupees.

Shobharam doesn't bother to put on his slippers fashioned out of discarded tyres. Absentmindedly, he puts on the trader's shoes and leaves. As he goes out, he finds a wooden packing box full of packets of salted biscuits. Shobharam quickly grabs two packets and hides them under his wrap. Along with a handful of bay leaves and a ball of local soap. One has to make do with whatever is available.

Shobharam narrowly escapes his father. Bhelu has been talking to Nodia in front of the vegetable stalls. A few vegetable vendors are waiting for customers with their ware of potatoes, aubergines and cauliflowers, in the faint glimmer of kerosene lamps. Business means waiting, waiting eternally. Shobharam hates business. The new shoes pinch him. If he walked any distance in these, there were sure to be blisters. A limping Shobharam melts into the darkness behind the fishmongers' stalls.

The slipper has got torn for the eighth time. The cobbler's shop is on the other side of the market, still some distance away. Nodia lifts his slipper and observes it keenly in the glimmer of a vegetable seller's kerosene lamp. It hasn't got torn at a new place, an old stitch has given way. The twine makers are cheats: they sell such flimsy thread these days that snaps with even a gentle breeze. Nodia turns the slipper around: the heel is nearly worn out. Soon, he would have to buy a new pair. Shoes are costly! The torn slipper reminds him that Fate always conspires against him. In this marketplace, no one is as ill-fated as he is.

The cobbler's digs at the end of the vegetable market are more like a hole. In between a steel godown and a shop that sells husk, Sitaram has been living in a burrow under a veranda for the last forty years. The small space is full of shoes, all of them old. For the purpose of decoration, Sitaram has hung a row of shoes in front of his shop. He never had a wife, so the question of children doesn't arise. He lives, cooks and has his meals surrounded by shoes. A really ancient fellow. Sitting in his den, he keenly observes customers with vulture eyes.

As Nodia, his torn slipper in hand, bent down to talk to the cobbler, an old boot hit him on the forehead. He was perhaps destined to be at the receiving end at all times! In disgust, he butted it back.

Sitaram was cutting leather with a chisel. From time to time, he sharpened his chisel on a worn-out block of wood. When he looked up, Nodia said, 'Please see what you can do with this.'

Sitaram knew, Nodia was worthless as a customer. So he took his time to complete what he was doing, spat out a little chewing tobacco and taking the rubber slipper, said with a wrinkled brow, 'Only beggars wear such slippers, where did you find it?'

An angry Nodia said, 'You talk too much. That's why you couldn't go up in life! Put a few stitches on it.'

Sitaram shook his head, 'Where? There's no rubber left. Please throw it away, buy a new pair.'

Nodia checked his pocket. He knew there would be no money. He pleaded, 'Please do something, I'll send you five paise after going back to my shop.'

Sitaram pierced the slipper with a needle and pulled back a twine. And said, 'Watch out, Nodia babu. If you bend so much, you'd be hit by the shoes.'

'I already have been', said an irritated Nodia.

Sitaram punctured the spongy rubber and said, 'The rich don't know how to bend. That's why they are hit by shoes.'

'Oh! What a philosopher!' Nodia put on the slippers and walked off like a hero.

The day continues to be bad for Nodia. He finds his wife standing in front of the hay-cutting mill. Earlier, he couldn't stand the sight, but he has got used to it now. She looks frightening. The short hair on her head is neatly parted, like a man's; she's wearing dhoti-kurta and a wristwatch. Sans whiskers, she reminds one of a prematurely aged boy. She wasn't unattractive when she was a woman. These days, she wraps up her breasts tightly. There are no visible signs of womanhood.

On seeing his wife, Nodia heaves a doleful sigh and turns his gaze away. It started almost a year ago. As he slept one night, he had a nightmare. One doesn't even dream of nice things when one goes through a bad patch. In the middle of the nightmare, he woke up on being kicked severely. He watched open-mouthed as his wife yelled, 'Arise from your slumber, you worthless Nodia!' She had cropped off her long hair with a large pair of scissors and long strands of hair lay about like so many dead snakes. She had put on one of Nodia's dhotis and had a singlet for a top. As Nodia woke up, she said, brandishing the scissors, 'Beware! Never ever shall you think I am a woman! Goddess Kali has appeared before me, and I am her devotee. Nodia jumped up to catch his wife by the hair, but couldn't. For one thing, the cropped hair offered no grip. Besides, she held the scissors and Nodia didn't consider it prudent to get too close. Since that night, his wife, Mandakini, had become a man. She continues to live in Nodia's house and is supported by him, but they have no conjugal life. Neighbours advised Nodia to get her treated by a good doctor, but that would mean expenses and huge ones at that. So Nodia has tried with the local homeopath. But how would he make her take the medicines? Mandakini is armed with a pair of scissors at all times. She wouldn't hesitate using them if he tried to get anywhere close. As she stands in front of the hay-cutting mill, Nodia knows the scissors would be stuck in her waistband.

Nodia tried his best to slink away avoiding Mandakini's gaze. But times are bad. That wretched Sitaram has become his creditor for five paise. If Nodia has to finally discard the slippers and buy a new one, those five paise would go down the drain.

'Hark! Nodia', called his wife. Nodia pretended not to hear and tried to get away. But Mandakini shouted, 'Listen to me, otherwise I'll create trouble.'

Just like a woman! She was spoiling for a fight. Still, Nodia tried to avoid her. Recently, she had been ordained: a temple should be constructed on Raja Fakirchand's hillock! She often received such messages in her dreams. Which fool would take her seriously?

Mandakini grabbed his shirt from behind and said, 'Will you go to hell with your money? You have no offspring, you wretched fellow. You'll die a miserable death. Since when have I been asking you for ten thousand rupees for building a temple?'

A brainwave flashed across Nodia's mind. He turned around quickly and said, 'So what if I don't have an offspring yet? I will have one.'

'You will?' Mandakini gaped in surprise. She searched her waistband, perhaps for the scissors.

'Of course, I will. Have seen a girl in the town. Getting married next Baisakh. Watch out and see the fun! Not everyone is barren like you!'

Mandakini was so flummoxed that she couldn't even take out the scissors! Her grip on Nodia's shirt slackened. He walked off merrily.

Nodia is indeed star-crossed. On reaching his shop, he found that good-for-nothing son of Bheluram sitting on a bench, sipping tea from an earthen cup. The scene reminded Nodia of the depth of his sorrow. The tea would be on the house. Shobharam was the worst scoundrel around. He would drink the tea, jot down the amount in Nodia's account book, but never pay up. Nodia couldn't be too tough, he and his gang might rob the shop in the night.

Nodia took the vintage coarse wrap off his body and folded it neatly. After washing his feet, he sat down behind a cashbox on a platform. He lit a few incense sticks and for a long time prayed to an idol of Ganesh: "Let better sense prevail upon humankind!"

There weren't many customers in the winter evening. The shop was almost empty.

Even before Nodia could finish saying his prayers, the wretched Shobharam had the cheek to taunt him, 'What's this, Nodiada? How could you go around in such a pair of slippers? For heavens sake, don't wear rubber slippers, they're bad for the eyes. Besides, can anyone from your station in life wear such dog-eaten slippers?'

Through the corner of his eyes, Nodia noticed Shobharam's new shoes. Motifs of fish-scales were embossed on the leather. The colour was nice too. Nodia alone didn't have anything nice. He let off the sigh that had collected in his chest and said, 'Bought this pair recently?'

Shobharam said with a flourish, 'Well … didn't exactly buy them, but …' He chose his words carefully; Nodia was unlikely to believe that he had purchased a brand new pair of shoes.

Nodia mocked him, 'Didn't buy? Was it a gift from your father-in-law? Or have you started stealing shoes as well?'

Shobharam swallowed the insult. He earned his living by manipulating people, and could not afford to be touchy. He said innocently, 'No Nodiada, nothing of that sort. Last week, I appeared as a witness in the sub-divisional court for Bairagi Mondol. I stumbled on the road and my old slipper got torn. So Bairagi bought me this new pair. But we were in such a hurry that I didn't notice that the pair was one size smaller. It's biting into my flesh. Please try them on, see if they fit you.'

So saying, Shobharam took off the shoes and pushed them towards Nodia. Nodia said absently, 'What if they fit? Can I afford such luxury?'

Shobharam seemed hurt, 'When will you change, Nodiada? No wonder your wife has become a man. Please try them on. If they fit, I'll give them to you for free. Bought for thirty, but such losses are a part of life. Please try them.'

That stirred up Nodia slightly. 'How much did you say?'

Shobharam smiled, 'Thirty. Don't swoon. These days, one doesn't get a pair of shoes for less.'

Nodia got off his perch and tried on the shoes. They were rather like formal shoes. The leather was soft. Nodia walked a few steps. Oh! didn't the shoes fit him! His feet were hurting this winter. The heels were cracked and infected. Dust and grime added to the problem. Besides, the rubber slippers offered no protection. If he stepped on gravel or potholes, he felt a shooting pain right up to his crown. Walking with the pair of new shoes, Nodia learnt what pleasure meant. His feet snuggled into their new homes. Neither gravel, nor dust, nor winter could do him any harm.

A visibly pleased Shobharam said, 'It's great, Nodiada. Looks like the shoes were crafted just for you. They don't look nice on wretched people like me. Better keep them. I would buy a pair of tyre slippers. On the other side of the market, Mahindar has set up shop with a pile of them.'

Nodia was in two minds. 'Are tyre slippers cheap? If they are, I too would rather ...'

'Oh no!' Shobharam cried out, 'They're awfully tough. You would get blisters in half an hour. And you wouldn't get rid of the corns in your lifetime. Those things are meant for the riff-raff. You'd better keep these. Give me anything, ten or twenty rupees, whatever you think is just.'

Nodia took off the shoes immediately, 'What nonsense, you talk like a thug! Spending ten or twenty rupees for shoes! My dhoti costs eight rupees.'

Shobharam fixed Nodia with a long stare. And then said slowly, 'Your hoards would ultimately go to folks you neither know, nor care for. Before you kick the bucket, try to satisfy the desires of your soul. You don't eat well, don't dress properly, what kind of a disease are you suffering from? The world offers so many dazzling ways for pleasure; you alone refuse to join the fun.'

Nodia protests meekly. But he is completely bowled over. He puts on the shoes again. They look gorgeous. And feel immensely comfortable. He last wore proper shoes when his father used to buy them for him. Since he was on his own, he has had to pinch pennies. Says he, 'But you're asking for ten rupees. That's too much!'

'When did I say ten? It should be at least twenty. Okay, okay, let's settle for fifteen. Even that would be almost gratis. It's only because they are too tight for me, and they fit you so nicely! Otherwise I could have easily sold them for twenty-five.'

'Twelve. And that's final. Collect the cash next month.'

Shobharam guffaws. 'Twelve? Better that you don't pay at all! Nodiada, Bheluram's son has seen a lot of money.'

Ultimately they settle for thirteen rupees. And it is certainly not a bad bargain for Shobharam. He had to dispose of the stuff as soon as possible.

Nodia conceals the shoes under his platform. One can never be sure – if the bloody Shobharam has palmed off stolen goods, Nodia could land in trouble. Let it be hidden. After some time, no one would notice if Nodia was seen wearing them. His assistants were warming themselves around the oven on the other side of the shop, Nodia hopes they haven't heard anything. Nothing works smoothly for him. Misfortune seems to haunt him ... Nodia heaves a sigh. And observes the pair of shoes through the corner of his eyes. He smiles a cunning smile. It has been a great bargain. Even then, thirteen rupees ... a huge dent in his finances. Did the shop assistants notice anything?

At this time, two rustic men entered the shop; they were greatly agitated. They ordered for rajbhog, singara and tea and started talking animatedly. The discussion was about how one of them had lost his shoes in Bheluram's store. The one who lost his shoes was wearing Shobharam's cheap, dirty slippers. Nodia listened, ears pricked. His hunch had proved correct.

Oh! What an ill-fated person he is! He looks askance at the shoes again. They are there.

When Sreepati was about to leave at seven thirty, he saw King Kong coming in from the dark. A massive boy of twenty-two years, tall and well-built, this was Sreepati's student.

Although he is huge, he is terrorised by his teacher just as a mouse is by a cat. Masterji speaks in unintelligible English and Hindi with equal ease. Khela doesn't quite fathom him.

The sight of King Kong annoys Sreepati. He looks at his watch and says in English, 'My time is up, Khelaram. Good night!'

King Kong simpers and says, 'Yes sir.'

A doubting Sreepati asks, 'Did you understand what I said?'

Khelaram takes off the comforter from around his neck and looks helplessly at his grandpa. Bhelu observes his grandson keenly through the opacity of cataract and says, 'Please respond to sir.'

Khelaram starts sweating. Sreepati says absently, 'Nothing can be done.'

This King Kong's father stole a pair of shoes just a while ago, right under Sreepati's nose. What stock! Sreepati shakes his head in disgust and fades into the misty marketplace. His head is overflowing with knowledge, but there is no one to whom he could impart his learning.

While leaving, he heard the old man scolding his grandson, 'Where the hell were you, you bloody rodent? Does it take so long to return from Beerpara? The fifty-rupee teacher waited for you and left! Son of a shoe stealer!'

The marketplace is quietly bathing in mist. A little faded moonlight has been seeping in. As Sreepati crosses the fish market, a mild stink assails him. Even now, some people are waiting behind their kerosene lamps with baskets of river fish. These people haven't read Shelley or Keats, haven't even heard of Shakespeare. They wouldn't know the difference between Marx and Tagore. But the wonder is that they too manage to survive. Are these just unnecessary frills that one could do without? He recalls the time when one of his professors explained: Acquiring knowledge alone doesn't lead one to the path of wisdom. A person who is well informed and who speaks on any subject isn't necessarily wise. If one doesn't have a worldview or a philosophical mooring, one bears the weight of knowledge just as a mule carries its burden.

Sreepati realises he has some shortcoming as far as worldview is concerned. His mind refuses to respond to the ambience of this marketplace, or the soft moonlight enveloped in mist, or the beauty of the lonely shireesh tree on Raja Fakirchand's hillock. He can't absorb anything much from the real world around him, although he is pretty surefooted in the world of books. He truly is well-read. No one in this area comes anywhere near him. He inspires awe among the villagers. Even then, he's aware, something is missing. Is it his lack of a worldview?

After leaving the market, he stops at a desolate place. He ought to exercise his mind if he is to acquire a worldview. He stands still and obstinately tries to soak in some feeling from the cold misty landscape around him.

It doesn't work. He sees no pictures in his mind's eye.

Suddenly, about half a dozen men are almost upon him, talking noisily. Drunkards all! Before Sreepati realises what's happening, Khelaram's father pops out of the group, and falls at his feet. He cries, 'For heaven's sake, Masterji, please don't tell my son about the shoes! I would go down in his eyes. I may be a dunce, but my son is highly educated!'

'Oh! Let me go,' Sreepati says with irritation as he steps back. Shobharam stands up, polluting the evening air with the reek of country liquor. Says he, 'Can anyone live like this, Masterji? Please talk to my father and son, I am clean now. Please ask them to take me back. I'll behave myself.'

Sreepati covers his nose with his hanky and shakes his head. The world is a rotten, stinking place. There is no worldview to be gathered from this wretched world. The world of books is infinitely more gorgeous.

The men are going somewhere with spades, pickaxes and crowbars. While leaving, Shobharam folds his hands and says,

'Bless us, Masterji! We are going to dig up Raja Fakirchand's hillock. Wish us luck.'

Sreepati says solemnly, 'Umm.'

Until now, lots of worthless people have tried to excavate Raja Fakirchand's hillock. They all hoped to dig out his seven pots of gold and lots of other treasures buried underneath. It is not a small hillock. Until now, it has yielded nothing better than snakes, frogs and rubble. Yet, some people start digging the hillock whenever they are flat.

Nodiakumar downed the shutters of his shop and started walking back, thinking of his plethora of misfortunes. Under his arm was the pair of new shoes, neatly wrapped in old newspapers. His old slippers made angry noises, perhaps in protest.

The whole place looks unusually pallid. The mist has dissolved in the moonlight just as puffed rice is soaked in milk. The half moon hanging in the sky reminds one of a ripe banana. Cold draught has been storming into the cracks in Nodia's heels. He walks with his head covered in the coarse wrap he had inherited from his father. As he passes by Raja Fakirchand's hillock, he sees a few shadows: a group of men doing something surreptitiously ... He walks faster. His daily collection is in his waist pouch. The times aren't good. And he is buffeted by one mishap after another. Despite everything, Nodia smiles a few happy smiles when he thinks about his new shoes. A nice pair, they are! He will start wearing them after a week. But if in the meantime there is too much noise about the stolen shoes, he will lose thirteen rupees. Perhaps the rogue had overcharged him. But he needed them. Didn't Bheluram say: even to beat one's wife, one needed a decent pair of shoes? Torn rubber slippers wouldn't do.

On reaching his house, Nodia got a shock. An unfamiliar woman stood under the hibiscus tree, face veiled by the end of her sari. Was she a woman or a spook? How on earth could there be a woman on his premises?

Nodia chanted the name of Ram and said, 'Who is it?'

'It's me.'

Nodia flinched for the second time and said, 'Me who?'

'Aha!' The female apparition moved closer. As she looked up, the veil fell off and moonlight caught her face. The soft light washed a feminine head with a masculine hairstyle.

Nodia choked. It was Mandakini, his wife.

'You? Dressed like this?'

Mandakini's eyes flashed like lightning in the moonlight as she said, 'As a woman, I am a spoilsport, am I not? You have chosen a witch from town. You'll set up a new family next Baisakh, have I spoilt the fun? Woe betide you, you wretch!'

While showering abuses, Mandakini nearly tore Nodia's shirt into shreds. But he didn't mind. Had fate turned the corner? A pair of new shoes and then a wife?

Late that night, Mandakini calmed down and started weeping. Until then, she had thrown utensils and mattresses around to express her displeasure. Nodia had observed her with fond affection. She had been exactly like this, loved a good fight.

When Mandakini started crying, Nodia said, 'Why cry, haven't you said enough? I am an unfortunate person, please don't cry.'

Mandakini cast a sidelong glance through her tears and said, 'How do I get back my hair now? I had such beautiful long hair. Will you love me without my long hair?'

'Oh! Shut up, you wench!' Nodia said affectionately, 'What difference does hair make?'

The seven drunkards have dug through the night and opened up a gaping hole by early morning. In the end, one of the spades makes a clanking noise as it hits a brass pot. The men start digging with renewed vigour. Then each of the spades starts clanking. 'Glory to Goddess Kali! Please bless us, Mother!'

The fading moonlight floods the minds of the seven drunkards. They flay their spades, pickaxes and crowbars randomly. The day is about to break. Perhaps the long night of Shobharam and his cronies would be over too!

It's coming out! It's coming out! As the earth is removed slowly, the thing takes shape. But what is this? They can't make out in the indistinct light. But they realise, it is not a pot, it's something much bigger. Is this the palace of Fakirchand?

The digging continues. They have blisters in their hands; even in the cold, they are soaked in sweat. But they are high on something entirely new!

The soft light of the dawn shows up the thing. The seven drunkards stand around it. The skeleton of an ancient railway wagon mocks at them. Perhaps it had been derailed long ago. The rusted metal looks yellow in the morning glow.

No one speaks. They are exhausted.

Bheluram has woken up his grandson early in the morning and made him sit down with his books. The boy reads English aloud, rocking slowly.

A bunch of worn-out muddy drunkards are returning by the road beside the store. One of them is Shobharam. He stops to listen to Khelaram's English. The boy has been reading real loud. Perhaps he will become a gentleman some day.

As he thinks of the prospect, a faint smile lights up Shobharam's lips even in this hour of distress.

A Class Act

Kanai always believed Bhaben Biswas was his father. Not legally though. Well, it was one of those things …

His mother Shefali has been working as a maid in Bhaben Biswas's house for at least twenty five years. Even now she works there. Bhaben has a massive household: three courtyards as big as playgrounds, contiguous mango and lichi orchards, scores of coconut trees, a vegetable garden, fifteen cows in a huge brick-and-mortar cowshed, rows of straw barns, a rice mill, a wheat grinder. And with all these, Bhaben Biswas rolls in wealth.

Legally, he has four sons and three daughters and Kanai obviously cannot be counted along with them. But Bhaben requires manpower to run so many enterprises. Therefore, Kanai too works with him as a labourer and gets paid with food by the day and a salary by the month. He has just turned twenty. He is not unlettered. Since he scraped through high school, he has been tagged on to Haripada, Bhaben's cashier-cum-paymaster. Bhaben himself told him, 'Learn the accounts, Kanai, you'd find it useful later.'

The accounts are prepared in the evening, after the day's collections are over. During the day, there is no end of work for Kanai. And through it all, he observes Bhaben's empire. Reckons he is entitled to a share of this empire. Not legally though.

Shefali is a simple, straightforward woman. She cannot keep secrets. Besides, bearing such a distinguished man's child is something to be proud of. One day, after a scrap with her husband Nayan Das, she in fact told her son, 'Are you the son of a second-rate fellow like him? Your real father is Bhaben Biswas.'

It may be scandalous, but it's not untinged with glory. In a way, Kanai was happy to hear this. And since that day, he has been checking his resemblance with Bhaben Biswas. His mother Shefali Dasi hasn't been untruthful. Kanai is tall and broad, bursting with youth and energy; his legal father, Nayan Das, on the contrary, is an ill-tempered midget of a man. The two don't go together. But try comparing him with Bhaben Biswas: Kanai matches him to the tee. Bhaben Biswas is a giant, tall and broad shouldered. His complexion is almost fair. Kanai too is like that. And he is relieved to discover the similarity. The sad part is that he has to call his father 'master'. But in his mind, he calls Bhaben Biswas baba.

Calling someone master publicly and father in one's mind is like standing on two boats simultaneously. It is not easy. At times, he confuses father with master, leading to unpleasant complications.

The other day, Rajab Ali of Munshihaat came with birds.

Bhaben Biswas's youngest daughter, Bini, keeps birds as pets. Cages of every description hang in the open space in front of their house. The birds make a racket through the day and litter up the place. The smell is revolting. It is his mother, Shefali, who cleans all that bird shit. The babu's daughter has her pets, the hassles are for others to take care of. This Bini had asked for a talking parrot. Rajab Ali brought one the other day. As they were chatting, Rajab told Kanai, 'I'm told you are a master of many trades, you can work as an electrician, repair pump sets, and you even know carpentry? With all this talent, why do you slog here for a pittance? A wholesale trader in Munshihaat, Mahadeb Porel, is looking for a clever man like you. If he finds someone really good, he'd pay up to two thousand. Why don't you try?'

Rajab Ali's suggestion merited consideration. Though not really first-rate in studies, Kanai has a way with tools. Starting from pump sets and generators, he repairs practically every gadget in this house. Bhaben Biswas's second son, Gobindo, has fixed a dish antenna on their terrace and laid a cable network for connecting local homes to television channels. Kanai is the one who does the technical work. Neither is he paid anything extra for this, nor does he feel sorry about it. He thinks, after all, it's a family venture.

Hearing Rajab Ali's proposition, Kanai blurted out absently, 'How can I go, Rajab bhai, leaving my forefathers' place?'

A stunned Rajab said, 'Since when did your forefathers start belonging to this place? Your father is from Nayagunj, isn't he? Why do you call this place your forefathers'?'

A slip of the tongue. Realising his mistake, Kanai tried to cover up.

Rajab said, 'Think carefully. Mahadeb has become old. He is richer than even Bhaben Biswas. Maybe, twice as rich, or even more. He is looking for a kind of manager. If you press, he might agree to pay you three thousand, not two. And you will be able to earn a lot besides your salary. After seven daughters, he has one son. That boy is still a kid.'

The proposal is indeed appealing. But Kanai sails on two boats simultaneously. Legally, he has no claim to Bhaben Biswas's estate; but morally, he too merits a share of this huge property and the business ventures. And this thought gives him a kick. Will he get such a kick elsewhere?

Himi pishi of the potters' hamlet had a problem: the hinge of her nutcracker had snapped. She caught hold of Kanai one day and said, 'Baba, please repair it. I have had it for the last thirty years. You don't find such sturdy things anymore. I promise, I'll pay you.'

The last part hurt Kanai's ego. He said, 'Why talk of payment? You don't have to pay me for such petty jobs. After all, I have gentleman's blood in my veins.'

Himi raised her eyebrows, 'Oh dear! Is that so?'

When he returned the nutcracker after fixing a rivet, Himi treated him with a great deal of affection. Then, after talking trivia for some time, said, 'Kanai, after all, you are a gentleman's son. Why do you slog like a domestic?'

Kanai fails to latch on to the hidden sting. Innocently, he lets on, 'Working in my own house, there's no shame in it, is there, pishi?'

Covering a sneer with the anchal of her sari, the old woman says, 'That of course is true. We too say, looking at Kanai, who would say he doesn't belong to a well-to-do family? He is tall, fair and has a gentleman's hands and feet.'

Kanai still doesn't get the drift, and smiles with pleasure.

Himi pishi offers him water and homemade nadus, and says casually, 'Make sure you get a decent share before the old man kicks the bucket. You have the right to.'

Kanai is a little nonplussed. Does everyone know the secret? That was a clear hint.

It was a matter of shame. And Kanai did feel ashamed. But it cannot be denied that he was also a little happy. The fact that people knew was definite proof that it was true.

Himi pishi continued innocently, 'So many are making their pile squeezing the old man, but you are the only one licking the dregs. Everyone says, Kanai is such a nice boy ....'

Kanai leaves after eating the nadus. But he does not think of demanding his share. Things might turn for the worse if he did anything of that sort. He is happy with the knowledge that his father is a wealthy man. And he cares more for this secret father, than his legal one.

After becoming a hunk of a man, he has measured, he is taller than even Bhaben Biswas by two inches. And it was easy to take the measurement. When Bhaben Biswas stands in the veranda to supervise his farmhands threshing paddy in the courtyard, his head levels with a place on a pillar where a chunk of cement has come off. Kanai has measured himself, using that point as the marker.

Of late, in the evenings, he too accompanies the cashier to Bhaben's office. On the floor are arranged separate piles of cash earned from different sources. Counting them, tallying them with the account books and the like is done under the watchful eyes of the master. As Kanai is much more deft with cash and figures than the elderly Haripada, Bhaben has apparently been developing a soft corner for the young man.

One evening, as Haripada left, Bhaben asked Kanai to stay back with a nod of his head. Then he asks in a sombre voice, 'How much salary do you get?'

'Three hundred rupees, plus food.'

'Not a small amount. And how much does Nayan get?'

'Twenty rupees a day, master. Plus food.'

'Oh God! That means six hundred a month! And your mother?'

'Hundred and fifty and food.'

'How much do they add to?'

'About a thousand.'

Bhaben heaves a sigh and says, 'So much money is flowing out, baap! That's why so little is left in my safe.'

It isn't true. Kanai is well aware how much money his Bhaben father makes. Around two to three thousand every day, leaving out the expenses. At the time of harvesting, the amount is five to six times more.

Heaving another sigh, Bhaben says, 'Let it be. After all, the poor are being fed and clothed. Don't you agree?'

'Yes, master.'

'These days, I have an acute pain in my left knee. Arthritis. Go and ask Gona to light the smoking pipe. After that, massage my legs for a while.'

Kanai is pleased with the order to massage Bhaben's legs. He may be a son, but the official relationship is that of master and servant. The massage gives him an opportunity to come close to his father.

As the sweet aroma of fine tobacco spreads in the room, Bhaben babu says, 'Your ma came yesterday, to plead for you. She cribbed a lot. But are you badly off? Will anyone pay you more in rural areas?'

He did not want to, but it came out despite himself, 'Someone is after me with an offer of three thousand rupees.'

'Aw!' Bhaben raises his eyebrows. After observing Kanai for a long moment, he says, 'Three thousand! So, what's the job like?'

'It's a manager's position.'

'What did you say? Who is after you?'

'A wholesale trader from Munshihaat, Mahadeb Porel.'

'Who's the fellow? What does he deal in?'

'I don't know the details. But he's a big businessman. Has farmland too.'

'Why should he offer you a manager's job?'

'He needs a clever man.'

'So, he thinks you are clever?'

'Not yet, he would test me.'

'What are your plans? Will you go?'

He did not want to say this. But someone from within forces the words out, 'Master, who would want to leave his forefathers' place? But, I may eventually go, if pushed.'

After blurting this out, he is surprised that the master doesn't respond in the expected manner. Bhaben either didn't get the drift or ignored it deliberately; he keeps smoking his pipe, which makes a gurgling noise. Then he asks, 'You don't have any brother or sister, do you?'

'No, I am alone.'

'Hmm.'

There is another pause. Then Bhaben pushes aside the tube of his smoking pipe and says, 'You work with Gobindo in his cable TV business. Does he pay you?'

'No, I never asked.'

'Why?'

'Well, I have learnt the work. And barda doesn't get much out of it. Not even half the subscribers pay regularly. Last month too, we had to disconnect three houses.'

A disgruntled Bhaben says, 'A fortune has gone down the drain. I told him, in the villages, people don't have enough to eat, how will they pay to watch TV?'

'They will, if the thing is properly organised. People want to watch those things even if they go hungry.'

'You think it has a future?'

'Yes, by and by. Most of the days, there is no electricity; people can't watch anything.'

'That is precisely what I said. Does such luxury have a place here? Let him try for sometime. Most businesses fail because of bad debts.'

'Yes, master.'

'At least, Gobindo is making an effort. The other three have given up even without trying. In which class is Botu studying?'

'Class eight, master.'

Bhaben sighs, 'He flunked last year. Not that there is any point in studying. It would be better if he joined some business. But the babus have no interest.'

Kanai knows. Bhaben has good reasons to feel despondent.

'And they don't care much for me either.'

Bhaben Biswas may be rich and important, but he does have a soft underbelly. None of his four sons cares a jot for him. It is an open secret. They are foppish and carefree. They don't want to soil their hands or waste their youth managing farmhands, rice mills and wheat grinders. And they'll do nothing so long as their father provides, for free, the good things of life.

'Do you know what worries me? They haven't learnt the tricks of the trade, they might squander everything after I close my eyes. I have no dearth of enemies. When I die, they would come in the garb of well-wishers and palm off everything.'

Every father thinks the same way. Nothing new about it. Kanai massages the knees of his secret father and official master with tender care and says philosophically, 'Why do you worry so much? After all, no one can defy destiny.'

Hearing this, Bhaben's knee starts. He raises his eyebrows, 'What do you mean? I have struggled throughout my life. My father didn't leave a paisa behind! I acquired all this after making so many sacrifices, and you say, it is destined that some cheats would enjoy my assets?'

It is beyond Kanai's ken to respond to such emotional outbursts. But he understands, Bhaben needs a little sympathy now, a little pepping up. At times like this, flummery works. But this evening, Kanai is apparently under the spell of an evil spirit. Despite himself, he has been saying things that he ought not to have said, things he doesn't even think of. He says guilelessly, 'But you have other offspring too. Why don't you depend on them?'

Bhaben had ignored the suggestion about Kanai's forefathers' place, but this seemed to hit bull's eye. He bolts upright, 'What did you say? What did you say, you rascal?'

Kanai says nervously, 'Did I say anything wrong, baba?'

Again! It was that same old confusion! Over father and master. The word father had inadvertently slipped out.

Bending down, Bhaben picks up one of his slippers and hits Kanai on the arm. Then he barks under his breath, 'You scum, how dare you talk like that? Get out, you son of a bitch, get out.

You're sacked here and now. If you even cross the shadows of this building, I'll cut you into two. Don't dare show your dirty face here ever again.'

If a man cannot keep his secrets, he is bound to be in trouble, sooner or later. Kanai could have hung on for all times if he could call Bhaben father in his mind and master openly. But that was not to be. On top of that, he had to face the ignominy of being hit with footwear. Whether it is the master's slipper or the father's, the ego is hurt if hit by one. The only saving grace is that a father's slipper hurts less than a master's does. Or that is how Kanai consoled himself as he walked out of Bhaben's house.

He did not want to tell the story to his ma, Shefali Dasi. But Bhaben's house is an open bazaar. Someone would have surely observed the incident. It didn't take long for the news to spread.

At night, his mother asks him, 'Is it true that the master beat you with slippers?'

'No, no, not too hard. Only once. It didn't hurt.'

'What did you do? Steal cash?'

'Oh, no, no. He just lost his temper, suddenly.'

'The old fool has become senile. You toil, sweating blood for him, and he pays you a pittance! I'll give him a piece of my mind tomorrow.'

'Oh, forget it! Don't do anything like that.'

'How dare he hit you with a slipper?'

'Oho, think that he has done it as a father, then you won't feel so bad.'

'Of course he's your father, but that doesn't give him the right to insult you.'

The news spread far and wide. Not only was the scene observed, some actually overheard the dialogue between Bhaben and Kanai that evening. And the rumours said that Kanai had asked for a share of the property, as a son.

People were delighted to discuss such a saucy story and it created fresh tensions in Bhaben's house. In the evening, Bhaben Biswas's wife called Kanai.

Somehow, Kanai wasn't scared to face her. He entered her room, holding his head high. Bhaben Biswas's wife was an emaciated woman; she was glum, but her eyes were sharp.

Fixing him with a piercing look, she said, 'What's all this about?'

Kanai lowered his head, 'I didn't say anything offensive. He misunderstood.'

She went up to close the door. And then, lowering her voice she said, 'Tell me, how much do you know.'

'What would I know? I don't know anything.'

'Don't try to be smart. Babu had many flings in his time. But I don't understand how you could muster so much courage! Did you claim anything?'

'No, madam!'

'Is your mother advising you? She's a stupid woman. She will do anything.'

'No, ma is not in the picture.'

'In olden days, wealthy people used to have many a woman. But that didn't mean their offspring ever dared to demand a share of the property! Tell me, who's advising you.'

'Madam, it's not like that.'

'What do you mean it's not like that? How dare you address babu as father?'

'It was a slip of the tongue. After all, the provider of food too is like a father.'

'Someone must be teaching you these lines! Let me warn you. Utter another stupid word, and I will get you murdered by Chopper Kalu. Do you understand?'

Chopper Kalu is a professional murderer, everyone knows him. At other times, the name would have been enough to frighten Kanai. But presently, he doesn't feel scared. He says evenly, 'Yes, I do.'

'If you even dream of getting a share of the property, it would be the end of you. Be careful.'

Kanai leaves quietly.

Two days have passed and Kanai has had nothing to do. Sitting at home, he feels his joints stiffening. On the third day, he goes out. Beside the cauliflower field in the palm grove, Netai is smoking a bidi. Seeing Kanai, he calls, 'Ore, Idike ai! You've created a big commotion. Sit down.'

Kanai does as he is told.

Netai says, 'There's nothing new about it. We knew, all along. Like a fool, you talked about it and lost a good job. You would've gained in the long run if you'd kept your trap shut. Tell me, has the manager of the rice mill, Tapan opened his mouth? Or the tractor driver, Madna?'

A surprised Kanai says, 'But what about them?'

'The same story, just like you.'

'What do you mean?'

'Do you think you're the only illegitimate son of Bhaben Biswas?'

Netai was laughing heartily. It was most irritating. Kanai said, 'Do you have proof?'

'Do *you* have proof?'

For the first time, Kanai does not feel proud of the fact that he is a son of Bhaben Biswas. He says, 'You're right, I don't have any proof either.'

'Then? Tapan and Madna too know about their origin. But they don't open their mouth. And it helps. In the end, the master takes care of his illegitimate children. But you crossed the limit. If you'd just kept quiet, he would've built a brick-and-mortar house for you, transferred some land in your name. The master isn't a bad person. And after all, blood *is* thicker than water.'

Kanai thought about it and it was clear as daylight. Although Tapan has a fancy designation of 'manager', he draws a salary of only six hundred rupees. Even he had built a pucca house last year. Madna's house is coming up too, at Goalpara. He doesn't earn more than a thousand as a tractor driver. Both of them are older than Kanai.

Heaving a sigh, Kanai leaves, with a bitter taste in his mouth. He is unlike them. He had never thought of taking advantage of the fact. He was happy with the thought that he was the son of Bhaben Biswas. That happiness has flown away, fluttering its wings like a swallow.

Three days later, Kanai started working for Mahadeb Porel in Munshihaat. Mahadeb is a straightforward person. Initially, he would pay Kanai one thousand rupees. After three months, if satisfied with the work, he would increase the salary to two thousand. And if Kanai could really impress, Mahadeb said, he could expect further raises.

The nature of work was more or less the same. Kanai gets addicted to work easily. He enjoys working hard. His new employer is happy with his performance. Mahadeb has invested a lot of money in different ventures. And it is true that he is wealthier than even Bhaben Biswas.

Kanai hardly noticed the days and months passing by. After one year, Mahadeb called him and said, 'I am happy with your work, son. From now on, you'll get a salary of three thousand. And, of course, a bonus during Durga Puja.'

Kanai does not worry about such things. He is immersed in his work. Very occasionally, he makes a quiet visit or two to his village, just to meet his mother. These days, he feels sorry for the mistake his foolish mother had committed long ago, for want of money or otherwise. He has no confusion about master or father anymore. He no longer thinks of Bhaben.

As Mahadeb was down with a cold one morning, Kanai was managing the office. Mahadeb's employees work under his supervision these days. And there is no end to his work.

At ten, an old man arrives, leaning on a walking stick.

At first, Kanai takes no notice of him. Lots of people visit them. The old man stands before him and gapes at him. Kanai says, 'Whom do you want to meet? Mahadeb babu is not well, he won't come in today.'

'I want to meet you, baba. I am Bhaben Biswas. Your *father*.'

Kanai stands up slowly and says, 'Please take a seat.'

It is difficult to recognise Bhaben. In the space of only a year, he seems to have aged terribly. After sitting down, he takes some time to recover his breath. He tells Kanai, 'With so many diseases, I am finished. On top of all that, I have other problems too. My eldest son fought with me and left along with his wife. The second has stolen his mother's jewellery and run away to Bombay or some such place. The third has failed in business. And the youngest, I hear, has taken to drinking. I am in dire straights.'

Kanai listens with rapt attention. Then asks, 'What are you planning to do?'

'I am on the brink of disaster, baba. There are conspirators all around. People try to con me day in and day out. I am told you have expanded Mahadeb Porel's business in a big way. Everyone talks good of you. Please save me, Kanai. Take charge of my farm and businesses. I'll pay you whatever you want. After all, you are *my* son.'

Kanai smiles. 'There was a time when I used to be proud of the fact. But that is not how I feel now, master.'

'I might have made mistakes, please forgive me. I am telling you honestly, they are nobody to me. These days, I feel that although an illegitimate child, you were the only one who had a soft corner for me. I have made a blunder, baba!'

'But these days, I do not consider you my father, master. There was a time when I was desperate to address you as my baba. But not anymore.'

'All right, don't address me as baba. But come back. I'll pay you a few thousands more than what Mahadeb does.'

'Will you give me a share in the property?'

'The law won't accept you as an heir, but I'll compensate.'

Kanai laughs heartily. And says, 'However bad your legal sons may be, however much they may ignore their old man, in the end they will inherit your property. And those like me, the children of your lust, would be left with nothing. The world is a funny place, sir.'

'Call me names if you wish. I've come to you as a last resort. Save me, please.'

'Do you know why you've come to me?'

'Of course, I know. I have come to seek your help.'

'That is true. You can hire many managers, but you won't get a devoted person like Kanai Das. You know pretty well, Kanai is your illegitimate child, he used to slog through the day to protect your interests, used to get a pittance as salary, but had never thought of going away. You did make a mistake in kicking him out. And you took a rather long while to realise it. Do you know why you want to take him back now?'

'Why?'

'You believe, once again Kanai will protect everything like earlier. He'll keep things in order until it is time for your legal children to take over. Am I not right, master?'

'No, no. Please don't think like that.'

'Master, there was a time when Kanai needed a father like you. But not now.'

Bhaben slumps in his seat, in a heap.

Please Look at Me

Please look at me. Yes, sir! I'm here. A little while ago, I jumped on to the jam-packed footboard of this public bus. Then, through the crowd of passengers, I moved under so many armpits and burrowed – like a field mouse – through the gaps between the legs of so many people to reach all the way here. The handle rods in the buses are high up, and I am too short to reach them; so as I stand, I grip the back of a seat and relax. If the vehicle jerks violently and I lose my balance, I let myself fall on the man standing next to me, but most of them don't complain, because I weigh so little that even if I fall on someone, they don't even notice it. At the moment, surrounded by mountainous men, I am holding on to the backrest of a seat in the rear part of the bus. These men have me so completely covered that perhaps I can't be seen at all! Or rather, even if I am seen, no one is noticing me. And *that* is my problem! I am often seen, but never noticed. The person beside who I am standing now, or the one in front of me, they are perhaps seeing me, but impassively. As if it wouldn't have made the least difference had I not been there! Perhaps it is because there is nothing in my appearance that makes me stand out. Yes, sir! I am five feet two; thin, but not thin enough for people to take note of; my complexion is dark, but not dark enough to invite a second glance. After forty, my hair has thinned, but I have not become bald; people notice baldies too. Above all, my physiognomy: it is neither handsome nor ugly – my eyes, my nose, my overall appearance, everything is unremarkable, nondescript. Therefore, as I am standing in this crowd, surrounded by huge specimens of humans, is anyone noticing me? The answer is, no, no one. Even if someone is seeing me, they aren't observing me. I know that.

A funny but sad incident took place shortly after my marriage. A few days after our wedding, I had taken my wife out shopping. In a few days time, we were to go to my in-laws' place for the customary after-wedding visit, and for that reason, a few gifts had to be purchased. As we left our house, I asked my wife, 'Do you want to go to New Market?' People from my station in life don't shop at New Market. I had always got things from the Refugee Hawkers' Corner down the road. Still, I made the offer primarily because she was from a small town and hadn't been to New Market. Another reason was that my in-laws were rather well-off. I suggested New Market so that my newly married wife would be happy, and later, when her people heard that the gifts had been bought from the most exclusive shopping mall in the city, their eyebrows were bound to shoot up. But the plan turned out to be a terrible mistake, because, if we hadn't gone there, this incident perhaps would never have taken place.

On entering the mall, my wife was dazzled by the array of glittering shops. She stopped in front of almost every store, observed the showcases with longing in her eyes and moved ahead only reluctantly. She forgot about me, completely. She was my newlywed wife, and it hurt. I tried to impress her by pointing out this or that, but instead of noticing anything particular, she seemed spellbound by the totality of the show. I felt awful. I slowed down, but my wife took no notice and went ahead, engrossed with what she saw. After sometime, I stopped, but she kept going. Her bewildered eyes were firmly fixed at the shops and she marched ahead, like a soldier offering a guard of honour. From a distance, I observed her walking under the glitzy electric lights through a throng of people. She even talked from time to time, assuming I was by her side, but didn't turn around to see if I was actually with her. After walking like this for some distance, she turned around excitedly on seeing something – in fact she wanted to show it to me – and stopped in her tracks. She looked around nervously, searching for me. At that point, I could not resist the temptation of having a little fun. In that maze that New Market is, I quickly stepped into the nearest corridor. Now, let this small-town girl try to find me! Let her pay the price for ignoring me. I smiled to myself as I observed my wife, anxiety writ large on her face, looking around and walking towards me briskly. Seeing her terrified face, I felt sorry for her, but still thought of prolonging the game for just a while more and entered another passage. And she, looking lost, moved on desperately, from one passageway to another, looking for me, totally lost in the labyrinth of the mall. I followed her closely. In the end, I realised enough was enough: she was looking frantic and was on the verge of tears. Tears were welling up in her red eyes. Therefore, I stepped up my pace, took a turn and entered the passage through which she was walking from the opposite direction. And waited for her, smiling. She walked towards me, came face to face, and passed me by at a distance of less than a foot, but didn't recognise me. I was stunned. Didn't she notice me? I took another path and quickly went to the next passage and stood under the bright neon sign of a crockery shop, waiting for her. Once again, she walked towards me, observing the people around her. Our eyes met, but still, she walked past and even after doing so, did not turn around to look at me. Like this, we met a couple of times – in front of a bookshop, a fruit stall and in the row of toyshops. But she did not recognise me even once, although she was searching for me anxiously! At that time, I had thought that this small-town girl was crafty, she had realised that I'd been hiding from her intentionally and so did not acknowledge me on purpose. But her anxious face, which was becoming more pathetic by the minute, said something else. In the end, I blocked her way in front of a watch shop and said, 'Here I am.' She looked at me for a long moment with astonishment. After that, she took a deep breath, smiled and said in a voice still trembling with fear, 'You! Where were you? I've been looking for you all over the place!' It was strange, but I knew she was telling the truth. On our way home, I told her that during our little game of catch-me-if-you-can, I had offered her several opportunities to catch me, in fact, had stood before her on several occasions. In the beginning, she refused to believe me, but when I insisted, she was greatly surprised. 'Really?', she said, 'Then you should never do it again. It was dangerous!'

'Conductor! Please stop the bus … I'll get off here … please, dada! … please don't … oh! my glasses …' As you can see, no one listened to me. The conductor rang the bell even before I could get off, the fatso blocking my exit didn't budge an inch, and the young lad in a floral shirt bent my specs with a neat jab of his elbow. That is why I was saying, no one pays the least attention to me – not in a bus, not on the road, not anywhere.

It's a pleasant autumn day, a mild sun is hovering in the sky. A soft sun and a gentle breeze have blended to create a tender day, like a purring kitten eager to rub itself against you. I am enjoying walking along the road. A little ahead, just after the crossroads, is my office. Look at this! The moment I get off the pavement to cross the road, the traffic policeman changes the signal. A stream of vehicles is blocking my way. Why, may I ask, my dear policeman? Didn't you see that I was trying to cross? Would your arm have become numb, had you kept it hanging for a few more moments?

The lift that is carrying me to the first floor is perhaps a hundred years old. With black cast iron grilles on all sides, it looks like a cage. Rattling from time to time, it moves ever so slowly. During the last thirteen years, I have been using this lift. In these thirteen years, the liftman, Ramswarup Abhogi, has taken me up six days a week. What do you say, brother Ramswarup, didn't you first see me when I was young, around twenty-six, when middle age was yet to cast its shadow on my face? Now, please tell me who I am. If I actually asked him the question, Ramswarup would jump up from his stool and say, 'Of course, of course, you are Arabinda Babu.' And he would be absolutely wrong. Never ever was I Arabinda. I have always been, right since my childhood, Arindam Bose.

I work in a bank. My office is on the first floor. Earlier, I worked in various departments, but for the last ten years, I have been in the cash section. I count currency notes fast and have a good head for figures. So I am not taken out of cash. Even if I am, I am brought back soon. For ten years now, I have been working in the cash section with utmost efficiency, at times in payments, at times in receipts. I work mostly at the payments counter as that is where more careful people are needed. I sit within a wire-mesh cage and close to my chest is a drawer with many slots. I can close my eyes and tell you how much cash there is in each slot. While making payments, I take out the notes from the drawer after counting them, close the drawer and count them again … After paying the amount, I put my hand through the hole for the next token, and after taking the token, open the drawer again, count the money and take it out … the cycle goes on. The people who observe me through the small hole in front of my desk may perhaps find my work dreary – they might say, 'Oh! How tedious his work must be, how awfully boring!' They see me through the hole, but don't remember me. Ram babu is one of our important and long-standing customers, he owns a large factory. Even our manager treats him with a touch of awe. Ram babu is a little finicky. Most of the times, instead of sending his employees, he himself comes in to cash cheques. Many a time, I have paid him cash, he has smiled at me pleasantly through the hole and thanked me. Once, my oldest brother-in-law came to Calcutta and went for a splurge. One day, he took me out to dinner to an upmarket restaurant in Park Street. I found Ram babu there. He was alone, with a glass of transparent gin in hand, eyes dreamy. To tell you the truth, I don't worry much about changing my fate. I never thought of taking advantage of my acquaintance with Ram babu. I walked down to his table only because I knew him for long. Ram babu raised his eyebrows and said, 'Where have I seen you? Just can't recall!' What with my brother-in-law watching, I felt awful. If the man refused to recognise me, if he was really stuck-up, it would be awfully humiliating. Desperate, I mentioned the name of my bank and added, 'I am in cash …' Immediately, his face cleared and sparkled like the drink in his hand. He said with a broad grin, 'Ah, now, I can place you. You know, I am so used to seeing you through the hole in that cage, and suddenly here … you understand, don't you! The important thing is the setting … Look at a man in an unusual setting, and you have nothing to identify him with. Just as you are with your cage with the hole, I have my suit and my bald pate. Take us away from that, and you'll find that we, you and I, have practically no identity. You see, just now I was thinking about setting, about background. I spent my childhood in a railway colony. My father was a tally clerk. In the railway quarters where we stayed in Katihar, a girl from our neighbours next door used to come to our house often. She had a stepmother at home, and was uncared for. In our house, at times she used to sit with my mother in the kitchen in front of the stove. She covered her knees tightly with her torn frock and helped my mother roll parathas. At times, she used to carry my perennially crying younger sister and comfort her. Ma used to tell me, "I'll get you married to her." And for that reason, I used to take a keen interest in the girl – I found her bewitching. She had a sad, angular face with rough undernourished skin. She had the beauty of a monsoon stream, as if she hadn't come to this world for staying long.' After saying this, Ram babu heaved a sigh and I asked excitedly, 'What happened? Did she die?' Ram babu shook his head, 'No, no, why should she die? I married her when we grew up. She is my wife. Now, she is huge, fat, bad tempered and keeps me in a tight leash. When I see her opening the fridge, rummaging through her ornaments, scolding domestics or asking the driver to take the car out, I cannot believe she is the same person, the same Beli, who gave a broad smile when my mother gave her two oranges in her sick bed. You see, today, I left the house after a big row with her. I was feeling awful, where has our old love gone? But sitting here, in this quiet corner, I recalled the old times, recalled her sitting before the stove, covering her knees. I recalled my mother's face, a face radiant with compassion for the wretched little girl. And once again, I find a tender love for her brimming over, just like old times. I'll make up with her as soon as I reach home … you do understand …' So saying, Ram babu took a sip of the transparent drink and smiled, 'Do you understand, the real thing is the hole through which I see you. The hole …'

The young man who has been waiting for payment absently tapping the brass token on the counter knows me. His father deals in old cars. Earlier, his father used to come to the bank. Nowadays, this boy does. Occasionally, when our eyes meet, I ask him, 'How's your father?' He nods politely and says, 'He's fine.' But I have a suspicion that if I am shifted from this counter and another faceless man replaces me, the young man wouldn't even notice the difference. Even then, he would absentmindedly tap the token, gaze at nothing in particular and if his eyes met the new cashier's, he would smile the same familiar smile. It would be sometime before he realised his mistake, because he hasn't really observed me. At the moment, he is perhaps thinking about his new girlfriend or planning to buy a scooter. He turns his gaze towards the girl at the reception desk and glances at his watch. He checks the number of the token and then through the hole, watches my weary hands counting a fat wad of notes. He fixes his gaze on my face for a moment and then turns away. But I know that he doesn't notice me. In another fifteen minutes, it would be two o'clock, time for the lunch break. I will lock my till and go downstairs. If he sees me then, drinking tea from an earthen pot and munching thin arrowroot biscuits, would he recognise me?

'How much are these bananas? Forty paise a pair? What nonsense! ... Yes, of course, I know it is martaman. Can't I recognise a martaman? That smooth yellow skin, the large size. One doesn't have to look twice to distinguish a martaman ... But I am not supposed to eat bananas today. I ate one only yesterday. I eat bananas only on alternate days. Still, give me one ... no, no, one would do. Please take twenty paise. Oh, What a lovely banana! Even after eating it, I retain the skin as a memento. I walk around for ten to fifteen minutes, holding the banana skin. People mill about me, unperturbed, expressionless. These people have never gone to war, never risked their lives for their nation or ideology, as a matter of fact, have never even performed one difficult task collectively. The country is dying slowly, but these people are walking about, drowned in their personal thoughts, disinterested about everything else. They have no sense of time. When they hear '1969', they only think of it as a number. Two thousand years of history doesn't come to their mind. For them, just as 'Telepathy' or 'Creak Row' is a word, 'India' too is just another word.

Please look at me. Me – Arindam Bose, a neither-short-nor-tall, neither-fair-nor-dark human being. I am neither telepathy, nor Creak Row, nor India – don't you understand that the words Arindam Bose are different from those?

Forget it. At times, a doubt creeps into my mind too – Do I really exist? Or, don't I? People thrust their hands through the slot in front of my desk and take cash. Some of them smile and thank me. But even if the cashier was replaced, they would thrust their hands in the same way to receive cash, some would smile and thank, but no one would notice the huge change that had taken place at the other side of the till! Please recall that incident in New Market – my wife is frantically searching for me and even though she comes face to face with me, even after exchanging glances with me, she walks past mumbling, 'How strange, where has he gone?'

I placed the banana skin on the pavement, gently. My dear Unconcerned Countrymen, if one of you step upon this skin, as you skid, you would suddenly come back to reality. If you are not grievously hurt, or if you manage to prevent the fall with effort, you'd realise that it has been a great learning experience and you'd look around and recall the name of the road along which you have been walking. You would reflect that had the accident been serious, you could have fractured a limb and the thought would remind you how dangerous your surroundings are, perhaps the dormant human being in you would wake up and think, just being alive and healthy is such a wonderful thing! And perhaps you'd be a wee bit more conscious about fellow humans and – one never knows – you might even recall that today, the sixteenth of July nineteen sixty nine, is your wedding anniversary – a fact you had completely forgotten – and also that you have crossed forty this year. Then, my dear fellow citizen, you would realise that in this country without wars and revolutions, I haven't done a bad thing by placing a banana skin on the pavement.

Are you thinking of the moon now? And of those three daredevil men? Please don't. Please don't worry about them. What's the point? People get worked up over these things unnecessarily and later, a time comes when they feel depressed. The three men have excellent machinery, they would land on the moon safely and return safe too. Don't get worked up about it and distract yourself. Please look at the road carefully. As you turn right after Governor's House, look at the beautiful, vast open field and the diaphanous sky. Look at the men who are walking around you, try to register their faces to the extent you can. In this beautiful afternoon near the Maidan, I am walking right beside you – please look at me. I have left my office a little early today, as I want to watch a football match. Looks like you too are going the same way, aren't you?

Look at that stupid boy! He missed a golden opportunity, being off-side. Only ten minutes to go and there hasn't been a goal yet. And that boy! Oh god! Who thought of giving him the red and golden jersey? Throw him out. Please, please shower your choicest abuses on him. Four letter words just don't come to my lips. But look, I too am trembling with rage. Since this morning, I have been worrying about those three daredevil men and my nerves are a little taut. And on top of that, a useless team is about to snatch away one point from us. One point, how preposterous! And only eight or nine minutes are left of the match. What do you think, would they score a goal? But how can they? All the players of the pygmy team have fallen behind to form a wall in front of their goalpost. And look at how our boys are playing! Who would think they have any intention of scoring? I feel like going down to the pitch and buttonholing the boy who blew up the easiest of chances by standing in an off-side position. I want to tell him, 'Look at me, I – Arindam Bose, I have supported this team since my childhood. I have made special offerings to the gods when this team won and have thought of committing suicide when they lost ... do you understand all this? You don't even know that I, a faceless man in a crowd, have been looking at my watch through tear-blurred eyes. Anyway, how does it matter to anyone else? It doesn't matter whether I cry or smile, or whatever I do. After all, no one notices me.

No, they couldn't score a goal. The referee blew the long whistle. The match ended. Kindly look at me now, shoulders sagging, looking pathetic. Just see how much I love my team, but it doesn't make the least difference to the players. They don't even know me. But after every victory or defeat, either I punched the air, smiled, hugged unknown men, or cried bitterly. For nothing! It didn't make any difference. Or consider the fact that I have been worrying about the moon and the three men – I couldn't even eat properly this morning – what difference did that make either?

Kindly look at me just once. I know, you're troubled about our team's position in the league table. Besides, you have to think of the moon and those three men. So many things are happening! Men are covering twenty nine and a half feet in long jump, presidents are being felled by assassins' bullets, the party you support is losing elections, revolution is taking so much time to come. And because of your preoccupations, you are paying no attention to me – Arindam Bose, a bank cashier, although I have been standing so close to you ....

There! Leaning against the railing in the first floor balcony is my four-year-old son, Hapu, an awfully restless child. Since morning, he has been nagging me, 'Baba, I want to see the chariot festival, please come home early. He is waiting for me. Under a shock of dark hair, his eyes glistening – I can see it even from this distance.

The moment I reach the staircase, he rushes down the stairs, excitedly. His mother shouts from upstairs, 'Hapu! Hapuuu!

Where are you?' Hapu gives me a broad smile and jumps into my arms, 'You're so late, baba! Aren't we going?' To tell you the truth, I am much relieved when I come home, when I am back with my own people. I hug my little boy. He has a lovely sweaty smell, his soft body is like the delicate winter sunlight. When I burrow my head into his chest, I feel I am having a refreshing bath. I tell him, 'Surely baba, we'll go. But I'm hungry, let me rest for a while, eat something.'

Hapu clings to me as long as I rest and keeps saying, 'Please hurry up, baba!' When his mother yells at him, I say affectionately, 'Please don't scold him, after all, he's a child.' Actually, I am terribly fond of the desperate way he clings to me.

A naughty boy! The moment we reached the fairground, he tried to wriggle out of my grip and run off. I said, 'Please don't do that, Hapu. Hold on to me. You can see everything even if you hold my hand. He looks to his right and then to his left and shouts, 'What is that, baba? And that one? And the one over there? I tell him, 'That's called the Ferris wheel. And that is the circus tent. And the one over there is the Well-of-Death.'

Hapu went up the giant Ferris wheel even as he kept munching his papad. There he is, high up in the sky, laughing and waving. He is coming down in a huge sweep of the wheel, and going up again. All along, his eyes are riveted on me.

Standing on the high circular platform around the Well-of-Death, we watch the motorbikes going around inside its cylindrical wall – up and down, down and up – with a deafening noise. Hapu clings to me as he sees the spectacle, wide eyed.

After that, we watch a circus show for half an hour. A man with two heads ... A singing doll ... an eight foot tall fellow. Hapu has stopped talking, but his eyes glitter with happiness.

I let go of his hand after coming out of the circus. He kept walking alongside me, quietly. Now, he has moved ahead. There, he is leaning down to see a pile of whistles at a stall. From there, he runs across to another shop where a man is demonstrating a toy aircraft. Then he moves ahead slowly, intently observing the airguns and colourful balloons ... he is becoming a part of the crowd ....

I was thinking about my team – we lost one point quite unnecessarily! Three men are zooming towards the moon. Will they reach there?

Suddenly I realise, Hapu is not to be seen anywhere. Even moments earlier, I had seen his blue shirt in the thronging crowd. I lost track within a moment. I shout, 'Hapuuu ...' and run.

Yes, sir! Have you seen a four-year-old boy in a blue shirt? His name is Hapu, he is naughty. Oh! You haven't seen him? He has a shock of curly hair, and mischievous eyes ... No, no, not the one standing before the doll shop, but he looks similar. No, I can't think of anything special about his appearance. He looks very ordinary, like me. I can only say his age is four and he is in a blue shirt. Yes, you are right, there are plenty of little boys in blue shirts, and many of them are four years old. No, sir! I can't say who exactly among these thousands of children is my son Hapu – I can't point him out precisely. And perhaps in this milling crowd, he too won't be able to find out who exactly is his ... you understand, don't you, his mother too couldn't, once ... If you see Hapu, please do tell him that it is me, *I* am his father. Please look at me. Please *do not* forget my face ....

The Bicycle

Ghotu doesn't care much for a wife, but he needs a bicycle, badly. Nothing can beat a bike. Jump onto the saddle as if you are mounting a horse. Then the magic of two slim wheels takes over – a magic that's truly wondrous. Looks as though you'd come down tumbling, but you don't. These days, Ghotu's world revolves around a cycle. And there is no dearth of variety among bikes. What a machine Madan Babu's son has bought! The colour is green, the handlebar low, and it flies like Pakshiraj. Haripada's cycle, on the other hand, has a fancy light; it has a gadget tied to the rear wheel. Just press the thing onto the tyre and, the moment you start pedalling, the light glows like an electric torch.

Not that Ghotu is particular about such frills. Like Nonte, he would merely fix a piece of pasteboard to the fork of the rear wheel. When he rides the cycle, it would hit the spokes and make a clatter. Just like a motorbike.

Although a wife isn't essential, Ghotu is prepared even to marry if a cycle comes in as dowry. But is there a prospective father-in-law in the entire locality who is capable of giving him a cycle? No one would give a daughter in marriage to a riff-raff like Ghotu. A bike as dowry. A pipedream indeed!

To put the record straight, there is no serious dearth of brides for Ghotu. There are plenty of miserable fathers of hopeless girls. They would be delighted to get rid of their daughters. If Ghotu wanted, he could get such a bride, in no time. But that's not on his agenda. It's a bicycle he wants.

Brojo Master however assures him, 'You'll certainly find a father-in-law who can spare the cash for a cycle. Just learn the trade, and then you'll see. A bicycle is nothing, you could fetch a sewing machine … or even a radio. But, for that, you have to prove your worth.'

Brojo Master is a famous tube well mechanic. If it's a question of digging tube wells or fixing shallow irrigation pumps, no one can do a better job in the entire district. He can dig out water, even in a desert. He charges reasonably, doesn't compromise on quality and never cheats his customers. And his expertise is required not just for new tube wells, but for repairing old ones too. As a result, he is in constant demand through the year. People run after him all the time.

It is not easy to become Brojo Master's apprentice. Just hanging around him won't do. He has a keen eye for people. He is quick to sack fellows who eat or sleep too much. He shuns the garrulous ones as also those who cannot get to the point quickly.

People fond of booze are out too. Only good workers find favour with Brojo Master.

Ghotu isn't sure if he's a good worker. Kanai Mondol is Brojo Master's brother-in-law. For almost three years, Ghotu was after Kanai. Efforts don't necessarily bear fruit. But Kanai has done this much: he's tagged up Ghotu with Brojo Master. Ghotu earns enough to take care of his meals and is even left with a few surplus rupees at the end of the month. That's all he gets presently. But, when he learns the job well and makes a name for himself, he'd be making a pile.

Ghotu is certainly after it. He is hanging on to Brojo Master like a leech simply because he has nowhere else to go. He comes from a section of the society where the father becomes a distant relative after the mother dies. In his case, the old man has even got himself a new wife. It can be said that that chapter is closed in Ghotu's biography.

Although the door behind him is closed forever, the one in front is wide open. All he needs is to learn the tricks of the trade from his guru. And he hasn't been doing too badly. The other day, Gorachand complained that his water pump wasn't working. Brojo Master was otherwise busy. He asked Ghotu to check and report remarking, 'I'd say you've got a hang of the job if you could identify the problem.'

Ghotu came back excited, 'There are some holes in the casing pipe, through which air's being sucked in. Looks like the casing's got to be changed.'

When Brojo Master went to check, he found Ghotu had been spot on. He patted Ghotu on his back.

In villages, the clients arrange food and lodging. It is not that everyone treats them like a son-in-law. Some show them the veranda when it is time to sleep. And in most households, the food isn't worth mentioning either. The workmen consider themselves lucky if they get a plateful of coarse rice, a little daal and a hodgepodge curry of sundry vegetables. But aren't there people with taste? Fortunately, there are. And therefore, at times, a solid portion of fish or a whole egg finds its way to Ghotu's plate.

On balance, Ghotu is a happy man. They have no permanent place to stay. They go around villages carrying pulleys, wrenches and bamboo poles that are fixed as tripods for digging wells. Life isn't dull either. The idea of a cycle had got stuck in Ghotu's head while he was in Peerpur. Peerpur is a big place, famous for a saint's mausoleum. Standing in front of Hareram Mustaphi's house, Ghotu was watching Mustaphi's fourteen year old son ride a bicycle. Suddenly, the boy asked him, 'Want to ride the bike? Go ahead.'

He was a handsome fellow. And it was so sweet of him. Does anyone make such offers these days? Ghotu was touched. But the hitch was that he had never ridden one. When he explained the point, the boy said, 'No problem, you can learn it. It's easy!'

Easy to say, but difficult to do. A cycle isn't an easy customer, it keels over either to this side or that. Ghotu struggled for an hour or so and fell down at least ten times. Although he couldn't master the trick, the cycle got into his head. And never came out ....

They are now working at Udaypur, fitting a shallow tube well at Mahim Mondol's house. From the tube well, a hose will have to be taken to Mondol's field. It is a big contract. They have just called it a day after it became dark. Mahim Mondol is a big farmer. In the evening, he sent a basketful of puffed rice and a few lumps of jaggery through a maid.

Gurupada, Sadhu Gayen, Taranath, Pocha, Handu and Ghotu are sitting in a circle and munching puffed rice. The jaggery is wonderfully sweet.

Gurupada is a skilled workman. He has been planning to get into the business independently. As he chews the puffed rice, he says, 'It'll be enough if I save another two thousand rupees.'

Everyone knows what it will be enough for. Gurupada's house and land had been mortgaged to a moneylender. He has been slogging hard to clear the loan and he is almost home. As soon as he gets back his land and house, he would start his own business. And he knows the trade inside out.

Ghotu asks, 'How long do you think it'll take to save two thousand more?'

'At the most two months.'

'After that you'll be a king!'

Gurupada says absently, 'There is no king in this story. It's my ancestral property, and I cannot afford to lose it. That's all. Only a wretch like me would mortgage his dwelling. There is only the house and three bighas of land – no kingdom. But I'll feel confident when I get it back. I will be able to hang on.'

'Will you continue to work as a tube well mechanic?'

'What else? If I make some money, I have plans to start a grocery. My wife can run it. There aren't many groceries in our village. Hari Shah runs a shop, but he is a cantankerous fellow. No one likes him.'

Chewing puffed rice, Sadhu Gayen says, 'You at least own a house. I don't, not any more. I sold off everything for my mother's treatment. And she died, nevertheless.'

'Where does your family stay?' asks Ghotu.

'It's a long story. My wife works as a maid in the house of a farmer called Naba Das. She stays with them, in their firewood shed, beside the cowshed. There is hardly any room. And I can't go there. I can see her during the day, but not after dusk. During rains, knee high water collects in the shed. Somehow she lives there, with two kids.'

Taranath was laughing. 'That's why I didn't marry. I was cleaned up after getting my sister married. I've to hang on. If Master kicks me in the arse and sacks me, I'll be ruined.'

Gurupada says, 'Oh, shouldn't worry. You are single, aren't you? You have to feed only one mouth; that won't be a problem. And you have learned the work too!'

'Tell me, is there any security in this line! Is there a shortage of tube well mechanics? And, do you want me to stay single all my life?'

'Listen, no one can deny a tube well mechanic his two meals a day. If you hang on, you'll never starve.'

Pocha and Handu are young. They aren't married either. But both have demanding families. Without joining in the conversation, they were discussing Hindi films as they munched puffed rice. They have seen one the day before yesterday in a video hall. Pocha, even while munching puffed rice, was trying to hum the tune of a popular song from the film.

Ghotu isn't a youngster like Pocha or Handu. He is over twenty-one. He too is single. He too doesn't have a roof over his head. But these issues don't bother him. The moment he closes his eyes, a bicycle floats in his mind's eye. It is true that human beings have invented many a machine, but a cycle is a cycle, it stands as a pinnacle of human ingenuity. And it is so hassle-free. Ride it and in a jiffy, vanish from the scene, and come back leisurely.

If Gurupada parts Master's company, there would be a vacancy. Sadhu Gayen would fill up that slot. Taranath too will climb one step up the ladder and fill in Sadhu's place. Then Ghotu will surely be confirmed in his job. And when that happens, he will earn more.

There is some confusion about the way Brojo Master fixes wages. He charges his clients a gross amount based on some rough calculation. And he pays the mechanics according to his whims. Gurupada and Sadhu Gayen make more money than Taranath. That's all right. After all, experienced people ought to get a little more. But by the same logic, Ghotu should earn more than Pocha or Handu, he is senior to them by six months. But who would raise the issue with Brojo Master?

However, Master is not a bad soul. He isn't mean in his dealings with workers. He is god fearing too. And works like mad.

In villages, there is nothing much to do after dusk. After eating the puffed rice, Gurupada spread a mat in one corner of the veranda and went to lie down. Sadhu Gayen and Taranath started chatting, sharing their joys and sorrows. Pocha and Handu left – they would see another video film. About a mile up north from Udaypur is Mehergunj, where there is a weekly market today. There is bound to be a video hall there. Pocha once asked perfunctorily, 'Coming with us, Ghotuda?' Ghotu didn't feel like it. There are times when the fights, the dances, the buxom beauties don't interest him. He would rather close his eyes and fly away on his dream bike.

He could see the cycle vividly ... the colour is moss green, the carrier is shining bright, the circular bell looks like a small steel can, the handlebar is a touch low. It's speeding away along the highway, with Ghotu on the saddle ....

Brojo Master and Mahim Mondol came out of the house, talking.

Brojo Master was telling, 'Can it be done in such a hurry, Mahim babu? We have only fixed the bamboo poles. Next, we will push in the wide pipe. Then the water pipe. It's not a simple job. It's Saturday today, no way can we complete the job before next Saturday. And I am not too certain about that either.'

Mahim Mondol replied in an even voice, 'I understand everything, Brojo. I told you, I'll treble the workmen's wages. Please do it. My daughter's marriage has been fixed all of a sudden. The wedding is on Wednesday. Complete the job by Wednesday morning.'

'Wednesday is impossible, Mahim babu. We'll have to push in three hundred feet of pipe, it's not a joke.'

'You are a master of your craft. You can do anything if you wish to. Work day and night. I'll pay four times the wages.'

'You can pay more, but that doesn't solve the problem. These are men, not machines. They'll die if they work twenty four hours a day, four days at a stretch.'

'But my honour is at stake, Master. The groom's family is rich. And they are adamant. The boy has come home from Gorakhpur. He'll get married and leave for his workplace immediately after the bou-bhat on Friday. I can't let go such a groom.'

'How does the question arise? Please go ahead with the wedding. We'll stop work for two days and start again when the function is over.'

'What are you saying, Brojo Master? Don't I have to show them my new shallow pump? They may be rich, but I am no less. The shallow pump will be sputtering, water will be driven right up to the overhead tank; and from there, water will be gushing down in torrents. The groom's party will be watching, jaws dropped. Only then …!'

'But moshai, you are putting me in a tight spot. Even if I agree, do you think my men will say yes?'

'Call them. They'll get four times the wages. On top of that, I'll pay them two hundred rupees each.'

Sadhu and Taranath have stopped talking. Gurupada too is sitting bolt upright in the darkness.

Taranath says, in a hushed voice, 'Did you hear?'

Gurupada's answer is a cryptic, 'Yes.'

Ghotu has no idea about how much a cycle could cost. Could it be less than two hundred rupees? Whether it was within two hundred or not, he saw a happy cycle tinkling its bell. It was eager to be Ghotu's!

Brojo Master called, 'Gurupada! Gurupada! Please come.'

Gurupada got up, and with him, Sadhu Gayen and Taranath.

Ghotu doesn't join in serious conversations. Continuing to sit in the darkness, he listens, ears pricked.

'Gurupada! Listen to what babu is saying. Can you do the job in four days?'

Bou-bhat: A ceremony conducted by the bridegroom's family two days after a wedding.

'Ten days work in four days! No way.'

Mahim Mondol said, 'My dear fellow, please try to find a way! Don't begin with the thought that you can't do it. If you can do it in ten days, you can do it in four too. Work longer hours.'

'Sir, we are only human.'

'Humans can do anything. They are climbing mountains, swimming across seas and what not! It's a question of my prestige!'

'Moshai, how much will you pay?'

'Three times what you normally get, plus two hundred as tips.'

'Excuse us please, sir, we can't do it.'

'How much do you want?'

'Please increase the wages by four times. Plus three hundred extra.'

'You are taking advantage of the situation.'

'No, sir. We'll have to squeeze out the last drop from our bodies. You can imagine what will happen to us if we work four days at a stretch without rest or sleep.'

Mahim Mondol has money and the arrogance that money often brings. Suddenly, he shouts, at the top of his voice, 'You *will* get it. Start the work right now. Must complete the job by twelve noon, Wednesday. The bridegroom will be here at five thirty. Before that, you must finish it in such a way that it doesn't look freshly completed!'

'It'll be done!'

'Start tonight. I am calling the electrician, Sadhan. He will draw up a wire and fix two lights.

'Yes sir.'

'Ghotu! Run after Pocha and Handu and get them back. They wouldn't have gone far.'

Hearing Taranath's yell, Ghotu dashed off. And as he ran, he thought: It would have been nice if I had a bike … oh! Just push the pedals and fly off!

Ghotu caught up with Pocha and Handu before they could cross the boundary of the village. On hearing everything, they too ran like mad. A war was about to be waged.

A seemingly pleased Mahim Mondol said, 'Excellent! Work hard boys, you'll have mutton curry for dinner.'

Brojo Master folded his hands, 'Moshai, please don't. If they eat heavy, they'll feel sleepy, they can't work. Better arrange for plain roti and vegetable curry. It would be easier to keep awake if the stomach remains half-empty.'

A plateful of mutton curry, rising like the sun on the eastern horizon, set prematurely. Ghotu started working with a caustic look on his face.

And the task was hardly easy. It was the month of Kartik, a cold draught was blowing in from the north. Spreading shadows from two large electric bulbs, the men started digging in the casing pipe. After swinging the hammer for only a few minutes, Pocha, Handu and Ghotu were soaked in sweat. But they didn't mind, the Mondol fellow was compensating well.

They pushed in four pipes even before it was dawn.

Brojo Master was watching them, sitting atop a mound. He said, 'Take a short break. Have a wash and eat something light. Then sleep for two hours. If you don't sleep at all, it'll do you no good. We have to complete the job. Who'd do the work if you're totally drained out?'

A basketful of puffed rice was sent out for them, not to mention the jaggery. Mondol had sent a plateful of steaming aubergine fries too, but Brojo Master put that plate aside. He said, 'If you eat fried stuff after working so hard, it would be the end of the story.'

Moved by their woeful faces, he relented and gave them two apiece.

There was rapid progress by midday. When their hungry stomachs were craving for food, the food they got was as per

Brojo Master's instructions. A watery daal with bitter gourd, some vegetables and rice. And boiled potatoes. Brojo Master insisted, 'You wouldn't be able to stand rich food. Better eat lightly. Complete the job first; after that, you'll have the wedding feast, won't you?'

After lunch, they slept for another two hours. Then they started again. Pipes were going down, work was progressing well. But by evening, Ghotu realised, his body wasn't too pleased. He felt sleepy, his limbs no longer had the super strength of old. But he went on hammering, hoping three hundred rupees plus four times wages would cover the cost of a cycle. Gurupada was slogging to make a part of his two thousand rupees. Sadhu Gayen to free his wife from scrounging. Taranath to find a bride. Pocha and Handu to make merry, also perhaps to give some to their parents. The shallow tube well of Mahim Mondol was digging deep into the earth to fulfil a wide range of desires. Deeper ....

Monday was the day of the weekly market in Udaypur. The haat was held in a field right beside Mahim Mondol's compound. Hordes of traders started converging from Sunday evening itself. By Monday morning, the place was bustling with noise.

Between themselves, Pocha and Handu griped, 'The food is no good. When you work hard, you need a little nutrition, don't you?' So, when Brojo Master had gone away to the fields to relieve himself, they went to the market and gobbled up as much ghugni as they could eat. Mahim Mondol has four buffaloes and twelve cows. Every morning and evening, it is quite an event when they are milked in a square behind the house. Pocha and Handu went there and drank glassfuls of raw buffalo milk. The cowherd was generous – after all, it was a serious project of his master and these mechanics were working real hard. He had no reason to be mean.

By evening, both were down with severe diarrhoea. There was no way they could work. Their hands didn't have enough time to dry up between their frequent trips to the field. To make matters worse, Taranath started shivering with fever.

'Eh!' Brojo Master's face was glum, 'Our boat is sinking just as we're about to reach the shore.'

Mahim Mondol said, 'I can give you labourers, but they know nothing of the job.'

'Give me a few men. Have to make do with them.'

Two labourers and Ghotu started again. By midnight of Monday, three hundred feet of casing pipe had gone in, but Ghotu's limbs were numb.

Putting in the inner tube is a tricky job. It has to be clamped firmly with a wrench. If even one pipe slips down and falls, they are done for. All their efforts would come to nought. This is a job for the skilled, can't be left to the untrained. Taranath took hold of the wrench despite the fever. Pocha and Handu too joined in. Handu said to Ghotu confidentially, 'My grandfather died of blood dysentery, I too have the same thing. There is a severe pain in my lower abdomen.'

They are working, seven to eight hours at a stretch, and then sleeping for two hours. But the rest seems to be doing them little good. As the pipe went down, Ghotu's hands – holding the wrench – trembled visibly. He gripped the wrench with all his might, gritting his teeth. The moment he closes his eyes, he can see the cycle … And his heart fills with joy … Moss green, low handlebar, a sparkling carrier ….

Ghotu came back to reality with the whizzing sound. Everyone was shouting, 'It's gone! It's gone!' The pipe had wriggled out of the wrench held by his sleeping hands and was whizzing down like a flash. Ghotu grabbed the pipe with both arms, as if his life depended on it. His arms were soaked in mud and sweat and the pipe had three more pipes joined at its bottom; it needed an elephant to hold it in place. Yet Ghotu hung on. If the others hadn't jumped to his aid, it would have been the end.

But Brojo Master did not scold him. On the contrary, he said affectionately, 'It is not his fault. He is a human being, after all.' Turning towards Ghotu, he added, 'Go and have a paan with zarda. You won't feel sleepy anymore.'

But Ghotu could not go for a paan. He looked at his hands through tears of pain – they were bruised and lacerated at several places. As he held on to the heavy pipe, a jagged joint of the casing dug into his palm and made a deep gash. Blood was flowing out of the wound like water from a tap. Sadhu Gayen took hold of the wrench and said, 'Go and put some crushed grass on the wound.'

That is what Ghotu did. It would have been a serious matter if the hands belonged to a babu. But there wasn't much cause for worry as they belonged to a mechanic. However, he was scared to sit idle. Mahim Mondol could object, My labourers are working and your man is sitting idle! I'll reduce the wage; after all, I have to pay my labourers, they don't work for free!

Ghotu mentioned his apprehension to Taranath. But Taranath said, 'No! Mahim is a generous man, he won't reduce our wages.'

By Tuesday night, when the entire pipe had gone in and the mouth sealed, Ghotu had large blisters on his hand. He punctured them with thorns from a lemon tree, removed the dead skin himself, and then put *Poison Killer* oil on his wounds. For want of a better choice, the poor respond well to such treatments.

Through the night, they poured water into the pipe. First water mixed with cow-dung, then fresh water. They went on pumping the water out. Everyone was taut with excitement. How was the water pressure, would it be enough to fill the pipe?

On Wednesday morning, mother earth flushed water through Mahim Mondol's pipe. It was clear and sparkling.

In spite of all his preoccupations among the bustling crowd that had gathered in his house for the wedding, Mahim Mondol came out and patted Brojo Master on the back, 'You have proved that you are a master! Amazing!'

The diesel motor pumped up water to the overhead tank. The household was flooded.

After finishing the job, they sit huddled in a corner of the outer veranda of the main cottage. In front of them, a big pandal has come up overnight on an open field. The wedding will be held under the pandal in the evening. The Mondol fellow is giving a huge dowry. Scooter, TV and so many other gadgets. And what a groom! He's a big shot somewhere.

A housemaid has informed them, this morning they will get hot bonde and two sandeshes each along with the puffed rice. And fried aubergines too. But none of them seems interested. They have squeezed out the last drop of blood from their bodies. All they are happy about is that the work is finally over.

Gurupada has been calculating. When he's through, he says, 'One more thousand will do.'

Sadhu Gayen is leaning on a wall, eyes closed. Says he, 'I still have a long way to go. Jatin Majumdar's plot is only two and a half kathas, but he's asking for ten thousand.'

Completely drained out, they talk listlessly. They would love to lie down and sleep. Suddenly, they hear a commotion from inside the house. Gurupada sits up and says, 'What's this noise about?'

Taranath replies, 'Such things happen during weddings. Relatives have old scores to settle.'

A little later, a flustered Brojo Master comes out of the house and says, 'Listen, there has been a disaster. Babu's daughter has eloped.'

Everyone sits up.

Brojo Master continues excitedly, 'She went to the well saying she was going for a wash. A lad was waiting there on his cycle. He picked her up and vanished with her.'

Taranath says, 'What will happen now?'

'What will happen? Mahim babu is in a shock. His wife has fainted. People have gone out in all directions looking for the girl. But even if she's found, it won't make any difference. The news has spread far and wide. Some people who had come from the groom's side for the gae-holud, have also heard the news. One could say the wedding is off!'

Ghotu, his back straight, says, 'Cycle?'

A flabbergasted Brojo Master says, 'Cycle? What has a cycle got to do with it?'

Ghotu gives him a broad smile, 'But just now you were telling us about the cycle. They have fled on a cycle!'

'Yes, yes of course. But how does it matter?'

Ghotu looks on, eyes shining. Really, what all can be done if one has a bicycle!

Gae-holud: A ceremony wherein the bridegroom's family brings turmeric and other auspicious things as gift for the bride on the day of the wedding.

I, I alone ...

When he finds the stub of a bidi in the ashtray, Diptimoy asks his wife Roma, 'Who came? Who smoked bidi in our house?'

'Your uncle, the one you call "Phul kaka". He came shortly after you had left for office; said he would come again.'

'Phul kaka?' As he unbuttons his trousers, Diptimoy furrows his brow. 'Strange! I don't remember anyone called Phul kaka. How did he look like?'

Roma feels a little uncomfortable. After slight hesitation, she says, 'He said, "I am Diptimoy's Phul kaka". Don't you remember him?'

Diptimoy shakes his head. 'I don't, because there was no such person. What did he look like?'

'Thin, old and poor … not a face you'd remember. I won't recognise him if I saw him in a crowd again.'

'Surprising! Hope he didn't steal anything. Did you check the room carefully after the fellow left?'

'There's nothing valuable in the drawing room. He was here for twenty minutes, he didn't go inside the house. He said, Bouma, please give me a cup of tea.'

'Did you make tea for him?'

'Of course I did! I gave him tea and biscuits.'

'Did he ask for anything more?'

'Only eight annas.'

'And you gave him?'

'Yes, I did. After all, he is a poor man. Said, he didn't have the bus fare for going back, he had come all the way from Haaltu to Uttarpara just to meet you. I gave him eight annas.'

Diptimoy looked a little upset. He said, 'Better be careful. Many Phul kakas are floating around in the city. Don't allow strangers into the house unless you are very sure.'

Roma did not think the man was a cheat. She said, 'There was no way of making out that he wasn't related to you. He knows many of your family members. He studied with your elder cousin. He had been to your house in Dhaka too. He said he had seen you as a small child. He was talking about the past. He even said when you were small, you had undergone a surgery for removing an abscess from your waist. It was he who held you during the operation. Pus and blood had splattered on to his dress.'

Diptimoy was about to tie the knot of his pyjama. He stopped halfway through and said, 'Strange! Am I making a mistake? I spent the first thirteen or fourteen years of my life in

Dhaka, and I haven't forgotten many things! Still, I just cannot recall this character Phul kaka! But see, the mark of that surgery is still there.'

'I know.'

'The man must be telling the truth. But I just cannot recollect any such person!'

Roma says with a smile, 'I am not exactly a simpleton. I don't trust people blindly. Maybe this fellow is a fraud, but he does know your family well. He said he would come again. If he does, you'd be able to recognise him.'

'Why did he want to see me?'

'I'm not too sure. From the look of it, he is in trouble. He might touch you for a loan, although he didn't ask for more than eight annas from me.'

Diptimoy furrows his brow again. He is sick of people who live on charity. Everywhere, from office to trains to house, the world is teeming with them. He hates the whole business of charity.

Roma smiles, 'People come to you because you are in a position to help!' Diptimoy looks at his dark and beautiful wife and is about to say something when she says, 'Let me bring you tea,' and goes in.

Diptimoy settles down in an easy chair. He does so every day, after office. He drinks a cup of tea, freshens up with a wash and then has another cup. As he relaxes that evening, he thinks about what his wife said: People come to you because you are in a position to help! That means, she too thinks he has surplus. It is true that he has enough. But he is not flush with funds. And whatever he has, came through hard work. His success is based on back-bending work, patience and an obstinate desire to succeed. And even with all that, he hasn't gone very far, although it is true that compared to his friends, he has landed on his feet rather early in life. Most of his relatives too are as badly off as they were. But at the age of only thirty-five, he owns a beautiful bungalow in a suburb of Calcutta. A few days ago, he has purchased a plot of land in Roma's name in the city proper. He has also taken a new life insurance policy recently. And he has lined up a few more things. He knows that many things can be achieved in the course of time. And all this should give a sense of security to Roma too. Why should she think he has surplus?

Diptimoy does not get excited easily, he rarely loses his temper. Patience and calmness are his forte. Even when Roma and Diptimoy were newlyweds, they rarely had an argument or misunderstanding. And it was so because Diptimoy was, and still is, engrossed in achieving happiness and success; he has always ignored the delicate emotions that stir up Roma. This evening too, he could have ignored it. But Roma seemed over-sympathetic about the man who introduced himself as Phul kaka. He had shamelessly asked for tea and eight annas, yet, why was she not angry with him at all?

So, when she entered the room stirring a cup of tea, Diptimoy fixed her with a cold look. Her face was impassive, her attention focussed on the teacup and she was preoccupied with many minute details about running the household. As she was leaving after handing him the cup, Diptimoy called after her. 'I wanted to ask you something.'

Roma turned around from the threshold.

'Are you a communist?'

She was slightly nonplussed on hearing the query, but in the end, said with a smile, 'What a question!'

Diptimoy managed to get a grip over himself quickly. He said, 'I was joking, please carry on.'

'You're strange! Why should I be a communist? And what do I understand of communism?'

'You are absolutely right! A rich man's wife should never become a communist!' said Diptimoy with a simple, uncomplicated smile.

Standing at the threshold, Roma hesitated for a moment. Saying, 'We should give something to charity for the sake of our children. Otherwise, we'll be cursed,' she left.

Diptimoy knows, Roma isn't dumb. She obviously guessed the reason behind his question. Before sipping tea, Diptimoy looks at the teacup. A whirl was going around a point in its centre. Diptimoy looked at it unmindfully.

The following day was a holiday.

Diptimoy starts working in the garden with his seven-year-old daughter Bubun and six-year-old son Pintu early in the morning. His house is in a compound measuring almost ten kathas. It is walled on all sides. By the side of the walls saplings of coconut and areca nut have been planted. There are also four mango, one jackfruit, one neem and two guava trees, besides sundry bushes, plants and a beautiful kitchen garden. It is winter and the vegetable garden is lush green with spinach, radish, and a few gourds hanging from a trellis. Diptimoy has two helpers who tend the garden and take care of his two cows. Through the year, the family eats fresh vegetables from the garden and drinks the milk of cows they own. And this gives Diptimoy immense pleasure.

Bubun and Pintu plant some saplings randomly, water plants and play with the soil. Then they vanish behind the foliage playing catch-me-if-you-can. Diptimoy observes the garden along with his two employees. He notices the lively ash-gourd creeper on the roof of the cowshed. Its large green leaves swing in the northerly wind. He reckons the creeper has grown too quickly, it is unlikely to yield much. He climbs on to the roof, a chopper in hand. From there, the view of his beautiful house and garden transfixes him. The building faces south, the front veranda is covered with an iron grille, it has four rooms with large slatted windows. Diptimoy plans to construct another floor; steel rods are jutting skywards on the terrace. Someday, when there are more people in his family, he would construct another floor. For the time being, there would be no addition to the family. Roma does not want more babies. So, as of now, the future of the first floor looks uncertain. When he becomes old, he would construct a room or two on the terrace, leaving a lot of open space. Lying down in an easy chair, he would look far away. Presently, he turns towards the garden. It looks sleepy in the shade of trees, he can hear birds chirping and the whirr of insects. Bees have built a hive in a high branch of the neem tree. Sitting amidst the ash-gourd creeper, Diptimoy feels a different kind of happiness. Beyond his compound, there is a road skirting the wall. He can see people walking on the road. Unseen by them nestles his beautiful house among trees. Immense satisfaction! He has carved out a small private world from the bigger world beyond those walls. All this belongs to him, and him alone. This house, these trees and these bees are his own, they are intimately related to him. Outside, people are walking on the road. They are outsiders, faraway people. Diptimoy watches for a long time. Pintu runs towards the cowshed, and looking up, shouts, 'Baba! I want to go up! Please take me with you.' Diptimoy smiles at his son and throws a length of the creeper to him. He says, 'Give it to your ma in the kitchen. Tell her, baba has asked you to cook it with mug daal.'

A chair has been placed in a clearing under the jackfruit tree. A newspaper is lying on it. Diptimoy unfolds the paper as he sits down, but doesn't read it. He keeps looking at his garden. Had the compound been a little bigger, he would have dug a pond. And in the pond, he would have bred fish. The house would have been fuller had there been more kids. Many stray thoughts cross his mind. He dreams. His mother is sitting in the cemented square around a tap, protecting her daler baris, which are being dried, from meddlesome birds. Her face is covered with the anchal of her white sari. He hardly meets his mother these days, rarely talks to her. Old age has caught up with ma, she is suffering from loss of memory; she cannot talk coherently either.

Diptimoy observes his mother, but cannot see her face. Suddenly a thought crosses his mind: he could have asked her if she knew someone called Phul kaka, and almost simultaneously, he recalls there would be no point, she wouldn't remember. His elder brother Mangalmoy lives in Kanchrapara. He comes here once in a way to meet them. Ma recognises him, but with difficulty. Diptimoy's house is so beautiful and thoughtfully decorated, but she hardly notices anything. She looks at things blankly.

Bubun comes out of the house with a cup of tea. As he drinks the tea, Diptimoy reckons, if Phul kaka was someone who knew their family intimately, he should have met ma. But he didn't. Normally, for people from their native place, it would be natural to enquire about old acquaintances, find out about lost relatives. The man did not enquire about ma. If he had, Roma would have told him. That means he did not come to trace old acquaintances, he had other designs. Diptimoy feels irritated as he makes this deduction; he hates scheming people. Roma may think he is extremely calculating, greedy, and stingy. But Diptimoy knows, he is not heartless. He donates to charities to the extent possible, helps people who are genuinely in trouble, enquires about the wellbeing of relatives and acquaintances. But no one can take him for a ride. Perhaps Roma has no idea about these things because she does not have to struggle in the world outside.

Diptimoy was sleeping after the midday meal. Bubun called him, 'Wake up, baba. Someone has come to meet you.' Waking up, Diptimoy finds, the day is over, it has almost become dark. One feels uncomfortable after an afternoon siesta. Diptimoy too feels a little numb in body and mind. Leaving his bed, he has a wash. Roma was removing the dried clothes from the clothesline. He tells her, 'Please make tea, someone has come.'

As he enters the drawing room, he finds the light has not been switched on. A shaft of brilliant red is streaming in through the window facing west, lighting up the whole room. An old man is sitting with a slouch, facing the main door. He has a wrap around him and a walking stick in hand. As Diptimoy goes around to face the man, he notices, the old man's face too had acquired a tinge of red in the evening glow. Even his small eyes appear red. He has had a shave just a while ago – his broken cheek is shining – but an uncared-for moustache hangs under his slightly crooked beak-like nose like a creepy caterpillar. He has a shock of black and white hair. The hair is long, it covers the nape of his neck. He is wearing a white shirt over a white dhoti. He would be between fifty and sixty years of age. Poverty has inscribed its indelible mark on his face, but he looks at Diptimoy without a trace of humility or timidity. On seeing Diptimoy, he straightens his back and says, 'You are Dipu, aren't you?'

'Yes, I am Diptimoy.'

The way the man shot upright, Diptimoy feels, had a touch of arrogance. He would have been strong and haughty at one time. Perhaps now, after being pushed around for years, he had become milder.

The man says with a smile, 'You wouldn't remember me. There was a time when I used to go to your house in Dhaka. You used to call me Phul kaka.'

What surprises Diptimoy is that this man does not fit the mental picture he had of Phul kaka. The Phul kaka of his imagination was a diffident beggar-like man. Although the man was old and thin, and looked poor in dress and general appearance, he was different from the description given by Roma. Diptimoy could not figure out what the difference precisely was. But there was indeed some difference. Diptimoy switches on the light to have a better view of the man and sits down facing him. Then he says, 'Roma, my wife, mentioned your visit. But I cannot recall you.'

'My name is Haren Ganguli. I studied with your elder cousin Ratan in Jagannath College for sometime. It was the time of the freedom struggle. I had to discontinue my studies.'

As the man is a Ganguli, that is, a Brahmin, Diptimoy wonders whether he should touch his feet. But Diptimoy is unsure and consequently, does not move. He has no recollection of this man. He says, 'Ratanda was much older. Almost twenty two years older than me.'

The man nods. And then says, 'There is another relationship; in a way, I am an uncle of yours. But that is too complex, people of your generation wouldn't understand such links. Besides, these relationships have no meaning these days. People who were close once have drifted away.'

Diptimoy feels the man is genuinely upset about the meaninglessness of relationships and begins to feel irritated. When old people start talking about olden times and bygone relationships, they don't stop easily. Diptimoy surmises in a clear and straightforward manner, he has no connection whatsoever with this fellow, except for the fact that both of them belong to the same society. Diptimoy neither understands the complexities of the family tree, nor its importance. He says slowly, 'I don't know anything, and I don't remember anything either.'

The man nods again and says, 'I can understand. Yesterday, I wanted to pay my respects to Ranga boudi, but your wife told me she cannot recognise people these days and finds it embarrassing to meet people. So I did not disturb her. If she were in good health, she would have recognised me.'

Diptimoy smiles, 'What if ma doesn't recognise you? You aren't telling an untruth.'

There was something in the statement; the man did not speak for a while. Then he says slowly, 'No, it is not untrue. But these days there are people who go around with fake identities.'

Diptimoy does not respond. He keeps watching the man, who suddenly takes out a dirty handkerchief and wipes his face.

He holds the handkerchief to his eyes for a brief moment and then removes it. He has pouches under his eyes; many lines crisscross his face. He says with a smile, 'I often took you in my arms when you were small. You were a lovely child. You used to be decked up with ornaments like a girl.'

The man becomes a little unmindful as he tries to remember a Diptimoy of yore. Then he says, 'I used to go to your house in Tikatuli. Then I went to jail as I was in the freedom struggle. I suffered much torture.' Saying this, the man smiles and adds, 'Of course, I too have tortured people!'

Diptimoy feels like smoking a cigarette, but is not sure if it would be proper to smoke in front of Haren Ganguli. At the same time, he knows there is no need to be awed by the man: he is a nondescript human being. Unsuccessful. Besides, it is clear, there was nothing between them that could be called a relationship. Yet, even after he takes out a pack of cigarettes and a matchbox, he keeps playing with them. The man does not even notice them.

Diptimoy asks, 'How did you find my address?'

The man, Haren Ganguli, smiles bashfully, 'It is not difficult to find your address. You have many acquaintances in Calcutta; you have an aunt who lives in Jadavpur. I go to see her once in a while. I even went to your office one day, but could not meet you. Then I thought it would be better to see you at home. In the office, you'd have little time to listen to me.'

'What do you want me to listen?' Diptimoy asks in a low voice. It was a simple question, but complex enough to create a cloud of uncertainty in the room. The man looks down for a long moment. And then, his head drops close to the end of the stick he was holding on to with both hands. Roma enters the room with two cups of tea. Bubun follows with a plate of biscuits.

The man was still hanging his head; Roma keeps a cup of tea in front of him and turns towards Diptimoy. Then she tells the man, 'Phul kaka, your tea.'

Haren Ganguli straightens himself. 'Bouma, I came today itself. It is a holiday; otherwise, I wouldn't have found Dipu.'

'You did the right thing.'

The man says with a smile, 'He doesn't remember me. He isn't expected to either. I was not that closely related, and the people who knew me are now scattered in so many places.'

An irrelevant point. Diptimoy feels annoyed. With an almost imperceptible nod, he asks Roma to leave. She says politely, 'You talk with him, I'll go.'

When she leaves, Haren Ganguli lets a sigh escape. Then, looking directly at Diptimoy, says, 'I am going through a difficult time, Dipu. In this old age, I don't get two square meals a day.'

Diptimoy gazes at the man steadily. The whole country is full of hungry people. It is old hat for Diptimoy. So, his expression does not change, he keeps looking at the man impassively.

Haren Ganguli adds, 'I married late. My daughter is only sixteen, both my sons still younger. To tell you the truth, I have no income. I cannot run my family. There is no point in telling you all this. You wouldn't like hearing it either. I have come to you as a beggar.'

Diptimoy no longer feels inhibited about lighting a cigarette. There is no need to show respect to this man, he is begging. Diptimoy taps the cigarette on the centre table and lights it. The man keeps looking at him.

Diptimoy asks, 'What do you do?'

'I have a petty shop at Haaltu. I don't have the money to buy goods. I have only a few cheap trinkets in my shop. It doesn't work out. Besides, I am not used to doing these things.'

Diptimoy says abruptly, 'What would you do if you hadn't found my address?'

The man sits still for sometime and soaks in the question. And then says, 'God has sent me your address. The whole world runs on connections.'

Diptimoy smiles, 'I too went through hard times. Those days, I didn't go to any relative or anyone for that matter, to beg. Whatever I have achieved, I've done so with my own efforts.'

The man is quick to agree. 'Yes, of course.' After a pause, almost as an afterthought, he adds, 'But age was on your side, and fate.'

Still smiling, Diptimoy says, 'You have worked for the country, but didn't you ever think about yourself … or your family? Isn't the country a collection of families after all?'

A sad smile flickers over Haren Ganguli's lips. He says, 'You're right. It is not that I've been able to do much for the country either. But I served a long sentence, underwent torture …. But I think in a way, even that was doing something. We hardly thought about ourselves.'

'But don't you have to think about yourself now? You said fate was on my side, but for me, fate means hard work.'

'True,' Haren Ganguli nods in apparent agreement, 'but we really didn't think of our own future. We believed, if the future of the nation was secure, the future of every individual would be secure too. Dipu, in our times, we had joint families. Not everyone was rich in those families, but everyone got shelter … and a share of food. It is also true that there was much pettiness and bickering. But basically, we learnt from joint families. We cared for even distant relatives. We learnt to share food.'

Diptimoy finds the argument irritating. He has seen much selfishness and dishonesty among the elders in his family. He knows, many of these people used to wear false halos of greatness. Yet, he does not show his irritation, does not argue. He only says, 'Yes?'

'When we fought for freedom, all of us thought in the same way. Nothing for oneself, everything for the people.'

'And what was the result?'

'Zero. People have become more selfish. Even then, I have a claim.'

'What claim?'

'I did something for the country. Now, let the country do something for me.'

With a smile, Diptimoy says, 'Then let the *country* do something for you.'

Haren Ganguli swallows the sarcasm and says, 'You too are a part of the country.' But he quickly controls himself and says with a smile, 'That was a childish argument. I said all this because you raised the topic. I haven't come to you as a former freedom fighter. Neither have I come to you as a relative. I adored you when you were a baby, and now at this old age, I am poor and destitute. I have come to you with the hope that you would be kind to me.'

Diptimoy sips tea, his brow furrowed. He notices, the man hasn't touched the tea or biscuits. He says, 'Please drink your tea. It's getting cold.'

Haren Ganguli picks up the teacup and says, 'You are not happy that I have come to you like this, are you?'

Diptimoy does not react. After a long pause, he says, 'You've come from a long distance, I must give you something as alms.'

Before he could finish his sentence, Haren Ganguli puts down the teacup abruptly and fixes Diptimoy with a steely gaze. 'Alms?' he says.

A surprised Diptimoy says, 'Yes, didn't you yourself say that you came to me as a beggar?'

'Indeed, I begged from you, but why should it be alms from your side?'

Diptimoy doesn't follow the drift, but loses his temper, 'If I gave you something, what else would you call it, other than alms?'

The last light of the evening had faded long ago. Yet, Diptimoy sees the glow of the setting sun in the eyes of Haren Ganguli. His jaw has stiffened, but he says in an even voice, 'God has given you enough. You've made very few sacrifices in your life, you have earned only for yourself, and maybe not all of it by honest means. I expected a little more respect and humility from you. Why aren't you ashamed of the fact that you live happily in a poor country? You'll give me alms because I begged?'

Diptimoy was stunned at first. There was only a marginal change in the expression and behaviour of the stranger, but it was enough to make Diptimoy's blood boil. He stands up with a start and shouts, 'Get out! Get out!'

Haren Ganguli too stands up. A crooked smile plays upon his face as he says, 'If ever a man held a knife to your throat and asked for everything, please do show him this anger, young man!'

He walks off without looking back, head held high.

For hours, Diptimoy tried to erase the memory of the encounter from his mind. He could not. The thought that a nondescript stranger, a beggar had insulted him in his own house was destroying his peace of mind. He cautioned Roma, 'Don't allow any stranger into the house when I am not at home.' It was not necessary, she understood. She did not ask anything, only nodded in agreement.

Late in the evening, when ma is eating puffed rice with milk sitting in one corner of the dining room, Diptimoy asks, 'Ma, do you remember anyone called Haren Ganguli?'

Eyes blank, Ma looks at him through her anchal, 'Who?'

'Haren Ganguli, a freedom fighter from Dhaka.'

Ma looks at him for a long moment. Then suddenly says, 'Natka? Haren was the son of our Sanatan Pandit, he was more famous as Natka.'

The name rattles Diptimoy.

Ma continues, 'He was a terrorist, fought for freedom. He used to go around with pistols and bombs. A dangerous man …

used to study with Ratan. He was jailed for murder. And when he was released, went back to his old ways.'

'He was not a good person, was he?'

'He was fine at normal times. But was dangerous when angry. His father too had been like that. Sanatan Pandit was killed by some people in a village in Bikrampur. Natka was then seventeen or eighteen years old ... Then something happened! What was it ...' Ma lapses into confusion for sometime and then says, 'Brahmins, yes they were Brahmins too.'

'Who?'

'Those who killed Sanatan Pandit. They were his disciples.'

'And what did Natka do?'

'He hacked two men to death in a field and shot another. The police could not catch him for a long time.'

Diptimoy needed no more details. He had heard many a legend about Natka. When he was small, Natka was his hero. He does not have any recollection of the man, but people used to tell him that Natka had been fond of him when he was an infant.

The information disturbed Diptimoy. The man had said, the whole world runs on connections. And what a strange connection Diptimoy had with him.

Haren Ganguli blamed him indirectly. He said things like Diptimoy had earned only for himself, didn't make any sacrifices, and so on. Diptimoy was in two minds about the person.

The whole thing had happened too quickly. Perhaps it should not have happened. On the other hand, it is plain as daylight that the notorious terrorist Natka does not exist any more. The man who came to meet him was a beggar. Perhaps he would have badgered Diptimoy again. He would accept money from Diptimoy and curse him because of his arrogance of poverty. Perhaps this little lesson would do him good. Perhaps the wretched fellow would do something better than begging in this old age.

At night, in bed, Roma tells him, 'I am scared.'

'What are you scared of?'

'Such a dangerous man. He may be old, but he was a terrorist once. And you had an argument with someone like him.'

'Oh! Don't worry. He is a pauper now, can't do anything.' Diptimoy turns to his side and embraces Roma. He kisses her lightly and says, 'The car will be delivered next month. And then, we could go for a long trip. Okay?'

Often, it is late evening by the time Diptimoy finishes work. He rarely leaves office before seven. He takes a taxi from Dalhousie to Howrah station. And then he takes a train to Uttarpara.

One evening, Diptimoy looks at his watch after completing the work: it is seven thirty. He has a mild headache. He feels thirsty, he hasn't smoked for a long time. He has a thousand things on his mind. As he comes out of his small office to the corridor, he realises there is no one else in their floor. All the offices along the corridor were locked. He calls the guard and asks him to close the main entrance. Then he starts walking down the stairs from the fourth floor.

Some distance below, he sees a man covered in a wrap leaning on the handrail at a bend in the staircase between the first and second floors. His face is covered with the wrap, which seems obviously cheap. Possibly a beggar. Diptimoy is coming down slowly. In the previous week, he had his blood pressure checked; it was high. It was not to be expected at his age. The doctor gave him a diet chart and advised him to avoid stress. Diptimoy smiles. The workers of his foundry in Howrah are on strike, his trading company hasn't been doing well either. He is running after two big orders from the government. He cannot avoid stress. As he climbs down the stairs slowly, he feels slightly giddy. He holds on to the handrail and absently looks at the man covered in the wrap, standing between the first and second floors. At times, Diptimoy thinks he is becoming greedy. He has made enough. He shouldn't mind if a few orders went to his competitors. Perhaps he should leave the business, go out and mix with people for a change. The next moment, he thinks he would construct a multi-storeyed building on his plot of land in Calcutta. Each flat could be rented out for six to eight hundred rupees. And he thinks of other plans too. And then he recalls, just moments ago, he was thinking of quitting. A shiver passes down his spine. No, he hasn't made enough, certainly not. He has many things to do .... As he climbs down, he notices, the beggar-like man has been standing still. Diptimoy goes down from the third floor to the second. He stops to light a cigarette ... the car would be delivered next month. An imported car, it cost him forty grand. He must go out on a long trip. Roma, Pintu and Bubun will be with him. They would go to Deoghar, Ranchi, Hazaribagh, Pareshnath. He would have to find someone to take care of his ma during their absence .... He climbs down. From a distance of three to four steps, he notices the man yet again. He is covered from top to toe in a black wrap. Diptimoy can see the dirty dhoti below the wrap and a pair of red canvas shoes. Hundreds of small businessmen have their offices in this building, supplicants and touts throng the place through the day. And there are beggars. Diptimoy passes the man in the landing. He is thinking of his car. A beautiful sky blue ....

'Diptimoy!' In a deep voice, someone calls his name from close quarters. He turns around with a start. It is the man in the black wrap. His face cannot be seen clearly through the hood, but it seems as if he had not shaved for many days. Diptimoy's heart misses a beat. He feels he has seen this face many a time in his childhood. He doesn't remember it clearly, but faint memories drift in from somewhere.

For a few moments, both men stand still. Then the man takes out his slender left hand and moves forward. Diptimoy is looking at his advancing left hand with an absolute lack of comprehension. Suddenly he notices the man's right hand coming out from under the wrap like a flash of lightning. Diptimoy staggers. As he watches with unbelieving eyes, the man plunges a sparkling dagger into his stomach.

'Ugh!' Diptimoy makes a noise as if he is hiccuping. The next moment, he wants to cry out, 'What is this? What are you doing?' but cannot. What comes out of his throat are a few sound-bytes of gibberish as if a dumb man was trying to talk. He could see the handle of the dagger protruding from out of his stomach ... at first, Diptimoy tries to lean on the wall ... he feels like throwing up ... there is a weight ... his stomach has become enormously heavy ... slowly, very slowly, his limp body leaning on the wall slumps down. His blank eyes could no longer locate the man in the black wrap. He is gone. Then Diptimoy regains his voice, and shouts, 'Roma! Roma-a-a!' Through the corner of his eyes, he sees people rushing in, from above, from below. Footfalls ... he closes his eyes in fear. The handle of the dagger is sticking out ... he realises he is being lifted ... perhaps taken into a car ... noises, people shouting ... there is a weight on his stomach ... heaviness ... the bitter taste of bile ... immediately afterwards, Diptimoy sees his garden washed in a coruscating green ... his own house. He is aware that such thoughts make no sense, but incoherently thinks that he is tearing off his plot of land from the earth and taking it away, constructing a boundary wall ... beyond the wall is a world unknown to him ... atop a roof, he observes unrelated, unknown people walking past ... they do not belong to his world ... Jealousy, tremendous jealousy – why should Diptimoy be happy? Diptimoy wants to shout, 'Why shouldn't I be happy?' ... He remembers, he has never helped anyone. He has only built a house for his family ... the people outside are too distant ... they are unknown, unrelated ... there is no connection ... no connection ... only Roma, Bubun and Pintu ... and he himself ... I, I alone ...

Slowly, Diptimoy drifts into unconsciousness ... someone stabbed him, but why? As a matter of fact, he could not enjoy anything ... the house with the garden seems so far away ... he did not even get to see his car ... there is a strong wall around the compound, yet, nothing is secure ... curses from all around are slithering in like snakes, they inject venom ... no, he isn't secure ... he cautions Roma, 'Be careful, Roma, be careful. Do not open the door to anybody, don't allow anyone to come in.' As he says this, he notices burglars crossing over his fence, the hoods are breaking down his main gate ... they are saying, 'Food must be shared. You have been snatching food for a long time.' ... Diptimoy gives up ... he sees a beautiful sky blue car whizzing past faraway places. From the other side of the windowpane, he is bidding farewell to himself. Diptimoy looks on ...

The Newspaper

The authorities say there would be enquiries to find out how and why the accident occurred. Enquiries are conducted. They say there would be investigations into aircraft crashes. These too are done. But they don't result in anything. In the end, it is announced that the tragedy occurred because of a mechanical failure, or human error. That doesn't bring to life one dead victim, doesn't join one severed limb. But, at times, the legal heirs of the dead get a windfall by way of compensation.

Just as Gouri did.

Why was there a flood? Why did the storm rage? When will people invent a cure for cancer? Why epidemics? Why did the building collapse? Why earthquakes? What was the motive behind the murder? Shyamacharan has been turning older by the day, thinking all this. A folded newspaper is tucked under his arm since morning. He unfolds it and goes through the contents minutely, whenever he gets the time.

Under the banyan tree on the banks of the river, Susheetal has set up a spice shop. The shop is made of latticed bamboo shavings and a thatched roof. Sitting in the shop, one gets to inhale the sweet smell of fresh bamboo stalks. A serried phalanx of bamboo stumps has been stuck into the ground along the edge of the river to check erosion. Boats moor at the wooden pier. Large boats, small boats. The boatmen leave their boats and come ashore. Porters unload their sacks. And load them on too. Passengers for distant places get onto small boats. Some of them open their umbrellas. Gusty winds blow in the pungent smell of the river.

One cannot read the newspaper peacefully in Susheetal's shop. The strong wind turns the pages into a tangled mass. Besides, there are some shameless fellows who, the moment you open a newspaper, would say, 'Could I borrow the paper please?'

Shyamacharan isn't too sure about what he searches for in the newspapers. But everyday, as he scans the paper from beginning to end, he does look for something.

People come to the spice shop from all around. Shyamacharan knows some of them well, while others are just nodding acquaintances, and some total strangers. Lots of people come to this riverside market. They bring in whatever they have to sell – potatoes, betel nuts, paddy, jute – heaped on boats. People jostle on the ghat. The traders then settle down in the shops dotting the river bank to catch their breath. They drink tea, chat and exchange business information.

Shyamacharan enjoys spending time at the ghat. He meets a lot of people, gets news from different parts, hears about places he has never been to, comes to know new characters. The spice trader treats him with much respect. He hasn't forgotten that Shyamacharan was, once, a judicial magistrate.

But, at times, Shyamacharan himself forgets the fact. His present life is like a deserted village that people used to throng once, one that used to reverberate with human noises. The people have moved away. Now, it is empty.

Gouri is Shyamacharan's eldest child, by his first wife. He has two more, by his second wife. His only son is a lecturer in Farashdanga College. He stays there with his wife and comes home once in a blue moon. He discharges his obligation towards his ageing parents by sending seventy-five rupees every month. The younger daughter, Parvati, stays with her husband at Nawabgunj. She too has little contact with her parents.

Only the eldest daughter, Gouri, is fond of Shyamacharan. She used to come home often from her in-law's place. Used to send money to Shyamacharan without telling her husband. Shyamacharan too was most deeply attached to his eldest offspring. Gouri's husband, Somnath, was an assistant sub-inspector of police. A nice boy. A god-fearing person and a kind soul, he was handsome, honest and courageous. In the Kharagpur section, on a dark night, a train slipped off its track and ploughed into the adjacent paddy fields. Six compartments overturned and twenty people were mangled into a mass of flesh and bones. One of them was Somnath.

But, was it Somnath? Shyamacharan still nurses a doubt. Somnath was certainly on that train. But his corpse couldn't be identified. A mangled body had indeed been handed over to Shyamacharan for performing the last rites, but it had no mole on the left cheek. Had the body been Somnath's, the mole should have been there.

Shyamacharan hasn't told Gouri the whole story. Had he done so, she would perhaps begin nursing hopes. As a matter of fact, even if it was not actually Somnath's corpse, one of the twenty mangled bodies ought to have been his. Had he been alive, he should have come home by now. He had been dead, and Shyamacharan didn't want to queer the pitch by raising the issue of a mole.

Gouri got a tidy sum as compensation. She came straight to Shyamacharan with the amount. That very year, he had completed the last extension of his service. He had spent the preceding six years of his career in this small market town, had even purchased a small house – that came cheap – here. He was looking forward to a quiet retired life when Gouri came home with a shipload of troubles.

Shyamacharan's wife is not unduly enamoured of Gouri. When she found Gouri had parked herself and her two children permanently at her father's house, she became rather listless. Since then, peace took leave of their household. Gouri is not someone to be cowed down by her stepmother. She has a sharp tongue. And her stepmother, Kshama, too has a piercing voice.

As a consequence, the tragedy has been wiped off Shyamacharan's mind and he usually keeps away from home. The little time that he stays there is spent with his grandchildren. And he expends a considerable part of his day searching for something in the newspaper.

Of late, his misery is complete. Gouri is young. She is at the most thirty-five, thirty-six and still looks attractive. At a casual glance, she doesn't look older than twenty-three, twenty-four. It is a rather dangerous age and, added to it, she has a running feud with her stepmother. These two facts have combined to create a peculiar problem: she has gathered around her a swarm of admiring young men. One of them is the second son of Binay Haldar, the wholesale trader of husk, from Kadapara. The fellow wears a wristwatch on the right arm, zooms in on a motorbike, talks incessantly with Gouri, guffaws loudly, and often makes off with her on the pillion. A tailor-made scandal for the small market town.

These days, when he finds no one else to talk to, Shyamacharan speaks to himself. Truth is, there aren't many who would spare the time to listen to the babble of old people. And from that point of view, the market on the river bank is a relief. Here, the river flows and so does time. Nothing is stagnant.

A farmer from Gobindopur, Mafijul, has come to sell his aubergines. As he drinks tea, he says, 'It hardly rained this year. Pests have screwed up my crop.'

The expression is deliberate. 'Screwing up' brings home the gravity of the situation.

'You and your crazy ideas! The dry spell has nothing to do with it!' says Haripada, a school teacher from Basanti, 'It's all because of these chemical fertilizers. More chemicals, more pests. This is all a trick of big businesses, growing pests with fertilizer, and making you buy pesticide to kill those pests. Two-way profit!'

Mafijul looks at Shyamacharan, 'What do you say, magistrate sahib?'

Shyamacharan has nothing to say. These days, he isn't too sure about things that happen in the world. He tends to believe whatever people have to say. He even nods when someone narrates an encounter with a ghost, his mind has turned so pulpy. And he keeps recalling, the corpse didn't have a mole.

Shyamacharan listens to his farmer companions and at times, joins in the conversation too. He spends the rest of his time reading his newspaper. He has a feeling he should find something important in the paper, something he has been waiting for so long. But the story refuses to appear.

Coming out of the spice shop, Shyamacharan returns home when the sun is directly above his head. At the Kadamtala crossroads, a bunch of Romeos have been chatting and making merry. One of them clears his throat and recites,

'In Posta, someone did confide
Your daughter's soon becoming a bride.
A fine groom will Gangaram make.
Don't you worry, for goodness' sake.'

Binay Haldar's son's name is Ganga Prasad. Shyamacharan bows his head and walks away hurriedly.

At the end of the market, he meets an elderly man, Neelmani Das. Neelmani is an idealist; he had participated in the freedom struggle and was an MLA once. He has been a good friend since the time when Shyamacharan was a magistrate.

Neelmani stops, 'Oh! Isn't it Shyamacharan? Which way?'

'Towards home, where else?'

'Wait a while, your home won't run away. I've to talk to you.'

Shyamacharan isn't interested in talking these days. No one says anything pleasant anymore. In a disinterested voice, he asks, 'What about?'

Neelmani lowers his voice, 'I saw the two of them this morning too. On a motorbike, going towards Kuthighat, just minutes ago. They don't seem to give a damn!'

Shyamacharan knows who the two are. So he gazes at the blue sky absently, 'Yes. Indeed you saw them. But what do you suggest I do? Hang with a noose around my neck?'

'Arre, Ram, Ram! Why should you hang yourself? But have you thought of a way out?'

'I've stopped thinking.'

'I even considered the option of getting them married. But your daughter is much older than the scoundrel. Besides, his father is furious.'

Shyamacharan sighs, 'It is my fate. Otherwise why should my jamai ....'

As he is saying this, Shyamacharan starts. Remembers, the corpse didn't have a mole. He hasn't said this to Gouri even to this day. It would not have been right. Shyamacharan might die one day and with him, will leave this earth, a vital grain of truth.

For some distance, Neelmani walks by his side. After

crossing the railway line cautiously, Shyamacharan walks homewards. Tucked under his arm, the folded newspaper seems eager to tell him something, but doesn't give away the message. After the midday meal, he would once again scan the paper thoroughly. He must find the news.

By the time he finished his bath and meal, it was late in the afternoon. Gouri hadn't returned yet. His granddaughter and grandson would be back from school soon. Shyamacharan tosses about in his bed. His wife, Kshama, having finished her chores, comes in and sits on the edge of the bed. 'We cannot show our face to people any more,' she says.

Kshama is middle aged. Life hasn't offered her much by way of comfort or pleasure. She has worn herself out working for the family. Nowadays, Shyamacharan feels sorry for her.

Checking the time on the wall clock, he says, 'Shall we go to Hardwar?'

'Let's go *somewhere*. Let your darling daughter be happy.'

'Who will look after her?'

'As if she needs looking after. She has a hoard of money. Has bagged a fortune after her husband died.'

'That's true.' He remembers the mangled, macabre face. Without the mole. Could it be ....

Late in the night, Gouri wakes up as she turns in her bed. A hushed voice seems to call her.

'Who's there?' she cries out.

Outside, in the moonlight, is her father. In a hushed voice, he says, 'It is your baba. Listen to me.'

'Baba?' A surprised Gouri leaves her bed. 'Why are you standing there? What's wrong?'

In the moonlight, Shyamacharan's face looks different. The sockets of his eyes are deep, overflowing with darkness – only the pupils gleam, reflecting the moonlight. He says, 'There was no mole on that face.'

'Which face? What are you talking about?'

Shyamacharan lets off the secret buried deep in the catacombs of his heart.

Gouri grips the window rods fiercely. Then, slowly, she turns to stone.

Next morning, Shyamacharan is back at the spice shop. The diaphanous sky breezes over the vast river. Boats sail in, boats sail out. All around, traders haggle noisily.

Shyamacharan sieves the newspaper for that very special piece of news. Doesn't find it. The traders talk incessantly, exchange facts and fiction. A pungent aroma wafts in from where the smell of tea mingles with the earthy smell of the river.

Gouri hasn't left her room since morning. Neither has she met anyone. Nor talked. She has been crying, all alone, in her room.

Shyamacharan gets to know of this when he returns home for his afternoon meal. Gouri is still in her room, crying.

Shyamacharan doesn't react. Kshama gives up after asking him the same question several times.

After finishing his meal, Shyamacharan slips in the newspaper through the window in Gouri's room and whispers, 'One finds everything in the paper. Why don't you go through it every day?'

Gouri takes her time. After a long while, she wipes her tears and sits down to read the paper, though she isn't very clear why she's doing it. Suddenly, she seems to develop an interest in the affairs of the world.

An afternoon siesta later, Shyamacharan tells Kshama, 'Ask the newspaper boy to bring in an English paper too from tomorrow. There are so many stories! One can't get them all in one paper.'

Death in a Dream

This is the way the world ends
Not with a bang, but with a whimper.

One evening, in the month of June, Makhanlal felt depressed.

That day, he had some pressing work in office and had worked long hours. When at last – after yawning and stretching himself – he got up from his seat and glanced at his watch, it was seventeen minutes past six. His back was aching, and from time to time, a nerve in his head was throbbing, like a flash of distant lightning. A piece of paper scratched against something in the air blown by a pedestal fan. Makhanlal couldn't see the paper, but found the sound eerie. The empty office around him looked massive. He felt that a fever had silently crept upon him through the afternoon, taking advantage of his preoccupation.

As he walks out, from the corridor, he hears the footfalls of the security guard, Ramjeevan. Ramjeevan was coming down from the second floor, hammering away his raw-leather boots on the stairs. The sound of his steps mingles with the clink of keys, coughs, and snatches of a rustic song. Makhanlal gets the smells that are associated with sealing this ancient office building every evening: the strange aroma of locks being sealed with shellac, the scent of old gum, varnish and wood. As he crosses the long corridor in partial darkness, he feels he has suddenly become much older. And he thinks, outside, a festival is coming to an end, without his being a part of it. As he climbs down the stairs, he clearly senses that the tune hummed by Ramjeevan has suddenly lost its way like a staggering blind man, defeated by the rafters, ceilings and walls of the building. The tune has died abruptly.

As he walks out and becomes a part of a thronging crowd under pallid streetlights, everything seems new and confusing, as if he has just woken up from sleep in the middle of a dream. He remembers, for a long while, he hasn't smoked, hasn't eaten nor had a sip of water. Normally, he should have reached home by now. Lolita would be waiting for him. But he does not feel like going home. For a very long time, he hasn't wandered around the streets of Calcutta or in the Maidan. While walking aimlessly, window shopping, and munching peanuts bought for two paise, he hasn't entered a restaurant on an impulse. These thoughts cross his mind as he stands at the edge of a footpath. Then he crosses the road slowly.

June has arrived, but the rains haven't. Heat is simmering from the cracked pavement tiles and the walls. The lights of

Esplanade have turned murky in the swirling dust. A tramcar goes past, almost brushing him, towards Bentinck Street. The pungent odour of leather from a tiny hole that was a cobbler's shop assails his senses. It is nauseating. Will it rain? Makhanlal looks up. He sees neither stars nor clouds.

Light and shade, human figures, rows of heads float in and out of his vision. Neatly arranged radios, golf clubs and shirts in shop windows. A mannequin in a suit flashes a smile at him. A cinema comes into view, with a lonely white weighing machine in its lobby. Makhanlal was going past. But as he walks away, he thinks of something and turns around. The evening show is being screened, there is hardly anyone in the lobby. He walks towards the weighing machine.

He drops a coin in the slot, and as it goes down a circuitous path tinkling all the way, Makhanlal observes the machine with keen eyes. The coin hits a lever and the machine suddenly comes to life as if struck by an electric current. A spring quivers like a nerve. Makhanlal reckons, the machine's heart, after remaining dormant for a long time, is now pumping vigorously.

A cardboard ticket drops into the ticket dispenser.

For a few moments, Makhanlal observes the machine and its smooth white coat of paint. It seemed to be sleeping. He thinks that after a brief interlude, the machine decided it was tiresome to remain awake and has gone back to its cold, unthinking slumber.

Makhanlal picks up the ticket, and sees a woman's picture on it. Under the picture was a prediction about his future with his weight printed on the reverse. He walks off, ticket in hand.

There is often good news for him on the side that contains the weight. Makhanlal notices, the weight mentioned is five pounds lesser than the last time. He was always underweight by three or four pounds, given his height. That means, as of now, he weighs eight to nine pounds less than what he should.

As the evening progresses, he feels more and more dejected. Usually, he does not bother about things like body weight. But in this evening of aimless walk, he realises that despite being a part of the city, its lights, its busy people and noisy buses, for a long while, he has been thinking only about his weight.

He walks absently for some time. And then, seeing a glittering cigarette shop on the other side of the road, he crosses over. When he holds out some coins to the busy shopkeeper and says, 'A pack of Charminar', he observes his head and torso on an impossibly long and narrow mirror in the shop. The reflection startles him. He steals a quick glance at his listless face and the shadow of fatigue and sadness in it. He knows he is not physically strong. But now, he looks anaemic. Has any secret ailment called upon him taking advantage of his lack of attention over the last few months? He is not too sure.

The shopkeeper keeps observing him even after handing over a pack of cigarettes and Makhanlal turns his gaze away from the mirror. Lighting a cigarette, he starts walking and wonders where he can go. He still has the weighing machine ticket in his hand. Before throwing it away, he reads his future: You will face danger soon, but it would be a passing phase. Danger? He wrinkles his brow. He could discern a vague pattern of cause-and-effect in it. He knows there is nothing logical about the statement, yet, he cannot ignore it. The coarse smell of tobacco spreads pitilessly in his throat and lungs. He crumples the ticket and flings it away.

After that, he walked for some time, without thinking, looking at the bright lights of the shops, the chiselled faces and the darkness at the depth of the alleys. Leaving behind the main roads of the Esplanade, he went around the maze of dimly lit lanes and by-lanes in an aimless way. He realised, there was no escape from the ennui; he was also aware that he had become extremely absentminded. Then he realised, he was terribly hungry and thirsty, his throat was parched. As he came across a decent restaurant in an unknown alley, he stood under its awning for a moment. Then he pushed open the glass door and stepped in.

From within the restaurant, a radio or gramophone had been blaring music with strange gusts of drumbeats. For a moment, Makhanlal felt the sound was telling him, like a barking mongrel, don't go in. There were several rows of electric bulbs in the hall. Light from the bulbs, reflected from the glass-top tables, steel ashtrays, cups and saucers and the polished furniture like countless shimmering needles pierced his eyes. He felt everything in the long hall was radiating light. In the restaurant, there were only a few customers, most of whom looked like foreigners and sailors. On his left, a woman stood still, leaning on a counter; it was difficult to guess her complexion through the heavy make-up, but she definitely looked pallid. She had dry hair and high cheekbones and looked like a dummy in her mauve sari. One of her slender hands was resting listlessly on the counter, waiting to be picked up by someone.

A few heads turn to glance at Makhanlal. Everyone present in the restaurant appears huge and strongly built. He notices some heavy, tattooed arms resting on tables. Some of the men were nodding their heads in time with the drumbeat. No one pays him any attention, and it looks as though he, with his thin frame, timid mind and blanched face has spoilt the robust ambience of the place. This music, the lights and the woman are not for him. He feels he has come to the wrong place and wants to go away.

A big man sitting behind the cash counter signals to Makhanlal to sit down at an empty table with a wave of his hand. The mannequin-like woman smiles through her overtly red lips. Makhanlal turns his gaze away. Nausea rages within him, he feels like throwing up. So he shakes his head to tell the man at the counter he wouldn't go in. The man puts a podgy finger into his mouth and starts rubbing his gums. He is still looking at Makhanlal but no longer sees him.

Makhanlal is not sure what he is doing. In his effort to go out, he gets hold of the glass door like a blind man. And at that moment, an old waiter in a flowing white beard comes and stands before the door. Makhanlal realises, the man has come only to help him. He turns his gaze towards the restaurant hall for a split second and sees a flash. A piercing look, a pair of blazing eyes, stabs him for a moment and slices away. Suddenly, a coin trundles down a winding tunnel through his spine and lung. And at that moment, the drumbeats roll down from a mad peak. For a fraction of a second, Makhanlal feels he is coming out of the trance, but cannot make out whose eyes they were.

The old waiter tells him something politely, his extravagant headgear casting a shadow on his face. Makhanlal does not hear him, or maybe, does not understand what he says. He feels there is a mystery about the place, something he has no inkling of. He begins to suspect that these people have set up a fake restaurant only to snare him. Simultaneously, as he casts another quick look at the hall, he feels he is leaving behind something important. He notices, in the lights and drumbeats reflected from a thousand gleaming points, there is a reckless resignation of soldiers marching out to battle. The girl has been leaning on the counter, frozen, the huge man behind the cash till has been looking at the ceiling, the old waiter has been watching him like an affectionate grandfather. But Makhanlal is not sure whose eyes he had seen. Someone cast a dagger at him silently and has gone back to their hideaway. Or maybe, it was only a flickering diamond ring, the reflected light from which caught his eyes.

What exactly did he see? As he pushes the glass door and steps out on the road, the discomfort lingers. He feels he has woken up just now and is trying to figure out where he is. He breathes with some difficulty, as it happens when one is greatly agitated. He cannot focus on anything, cannot make out what has been happening around him. His limbs are no longer under his control. Why did he come here? Normally, he should have been back home by now. At this moment, his wife would be waiting for him, perhaps lying down with six-year-old Buku beside her. When he goes back, he would see her unkempt hair and dishevelled sari as she opened the door.

For some time, Makhanlal walks on, lost in thoughts and uneasiness. The earlier stuffiness is gone now. It must have rained somewhere nearby. Esplanade looks unreal, the monument stands like the only surviving column of a ravaged fort. He is surrounded by strangers. He sees faces and figures, some of them reflected from showcases and mirrors and distorted into abstract forms. He wonders what it was all about, and whose eyes he saw. Whose eyes? Didn't they look cruel? The world would be a safer place if people with such vicious eyes ceased to exist. Makhanlal feels lonesome. Someone has been talking to him continuously through a tiny microphone embedded in his head. But he hears nothing. He cannot understand anything. From a thousand crevices in the sky, from a world of dreams and memories, broken, distorted and synthesised words and scenes shower upon him.

Or perhaps it is the rain. He watches the first shower of June, stopped in his tracks by the raised arm of a traffic policeman as he tries to cross Suren Banerjee Road. Millions of thermometers are crashing down on the tarred road.

He comes back to his senses and runs to board a bus going towards Sealdah station. It was an awfully crowded double-decker. He stops for a while under a bus shelter, where a crowd has already gathered. Jostled by the crowd and breathing in cigarette smoke and sweaty vapour, he hears raindrops falling like the light footfalls of a faraway herd of deer … everything has turned topsy-turvy around him …. The rain has been dancing down the road, along the pavement and on the roofs of moving vehicles, like sprightly deer. A policeman, tall office buildings and bright showrooms – all getting quietly drenched in the rain.

When the first gust of rain becomes lighter, Makhanlal ties his wristwatch with a handkerchief and starts walking. Soon, it starts pouring again. The sharp raindrops hurt him. His head gets wet in no time, countless streams of water slide down his shoulders like squiggly worms.

The road, quivering under a blanket of splattering raindrops, seems to be without a beginning or an end. A scooter cuts through the water leaving behind shock waves on both sides. A robust young man is driving it. On the pillion, a girl, her head covered with a scarf, is leaning on the man. Like Makhanlal, there are a few others who have been braving the rain on foot. The scooter goes away through the rain, turns suddenly, jumps up and vanishes from the scene. Makhanlal is surprised that it hasn't overturned.

There is nothing around him except the rain. On both sides of the road, tall buildings – one feels insignificant standing beneath them – have faded out almost completely; their helplessness reminds one of a watercolour painting of leafy trees cringing in rain. As a lonely Makhanlal walks, he feels the rain has been closing in on him like a shroud; the scene before him –blurred buildings, shops and a few hazy people on the road – is unreal.

Somehow, he too has been merging with the rain. Familiar streets seem unknown. The rain has been washing away his known world. It is as if he is standing before a screen: the moment the screen was removed, he would find himself in another country. Water has been flowing along the road in a steady stream by now, small waves break upon his shoes and flow away. But he does not notice it.

What could be more invigorating than rain? He recalls he has not drenched himself in the rain in a long time, and neither has he bathed in the sun. He feels he has all this time been sleepwalking through life bereft of love of nature. He has not turned around to notice the days. He never wanted to retain any memory. He feels, in the process, he has forgotten many a scene, sound, soundlessness, gaits of people and pains of bereavement.

From far away, someone was hurling at him the noise of a trudging tramcar, shouts of people, the whisper of falling leaves.

He has never been through such a lonely, friendless evening. Why did he walk out in the rain? Why? He recalls, he has many more unfulfilled dreams. He had always wanted to lie down under the shade of a tree in Curzon Park through a languid winter afternoon; that dream remains unfulfilled. He craved to go back somewhere, but did not wish to meet any human being. In East Bengal, in the courtyard of their old house, the morning flowers have withered by now … the pond covered with algae, its banks blackened by moss … wind whistling through kochu bushes … a solitary ghugu warbling from the kamranga tree to announce the utter hopelessness of the afternoons….

Whose eyes did he see? Did they belong to a complete stranger? Why does he feel like a destitute today? He has never gone through anything like this. In his childhood, he never paid attention to the periodic chime of their grandfather clock. But in the hours of solitude, or waking up suddenly in the middle of the night, when he heard the tick-tock announcing the clock's obstinate desire to uncoil its spring, he thought: Oh! It's the clock. Something similar has happened today, he suddenly felt terribly alone and desolate and it brought him face to face with agonies that had been dormant for years. Walking through a mist of sadness, Makhanlal reaches Sealdah station and boards the eight-forty-five local.

The rain had stopped, although the sky was gloomy. Through the windows of the compartment, nothing could be seen, neither stars nor clouds. Makhanlal rested his head on the window sill and allowed the rushing wind to play upon his face. The cold draught pierced his drenched head, neck and chest. The clang of the train changing lines, the sound of the couplings, and other noises from underneath the compartment kept disturbing him. In the ghostly window of a train rushing past from the opposite direction, a black arm slithered like a snake. On someone's spectacles, a morbid twisted reflection of the world outside flashed for a split second before fading away.

He returned to his suburban home a little late in the evening. Lolita looked disoriented when she opened the door – as if she was still sleeping. Briefly, behind her, Makhanlal sees three boats sailing towards a setting sun on a calendar. Buku is sleeping on the floor. After returning from a strange and confusing crowd of people, Makhanlal feels like a stranger in his own home.

After having a wash and eating his supper – which had been kept under a cover – he slowly returned to normalcy. As Lolita sat down to eat, she said something. He listened to her for sometime and then lost the thread.

He lies down on a cot and watches Lolita. Before stretching out on the floor beside Buku in a separate bed under a mosquito net, she was looking for mosquitoes with a small electric torch. He remembers, once, in a crowded tram or bus, he had seen a green tattoo on a fellow passenger's arm. It was a picture of a naked fairy. She had wings like a crow's on her back. The wrinkled skin of the old man distorted the fairy – her face was smudged. Makhanlal had thought the fairy had lived on that arm for many years, yet she was desperate to fly away.

Before he drifts off to sleep, he tells his wife, 'We will go for a long holiday when I am able to take a few days off.'

Late at night, Makhanlal wakes up as he has a nightmare. For some time, he stares blankly into the darkness without realising where he is. The disjointed sound of a scooter reverberates in his head. He realises, his limbs are stretched peculiarly. He is lying on his back and his hands are on his chest. Some people had removed the cover of a manhole and were lying in wait in a dark desolate alley – for him. He stepped into the maw of the manhole, which covered the entire width of the road, and was pulled down by gravity through vacuum and timelessness. He escaped narrowly. If he hadn't woken up in time, he would have died like a miserable rat in that dark, putrid hole.

An agitated Makhanlal sits up. He calls out in an unsteady and unfamiliar voice, 'Lolita!', but no one responds. He longs to hear the sound of a living human being. The night was silent, it had stopped raining, but somewhere, collected rainwater was dripping into a tin can. Someone was hurling the heavy sound of each drop towards him like an unwavering arrow.

For a long time, he sat between sleep and wakefulness, immobilised by a strange incomprehension. On the left side of his chest, an undefined pain was stuck like a postage stamp. He felt that the nightmare hadn't ended. The men were still waiting for him, and they were not far away. If he fell asleep again, they would once again drag him into the open manhole. The room jumped up before his eyes in a blue flash of distant lightning for a moment and then vanished again. What would happen if he fell asleep? The sound of raindrops falling into the tin can turned into a monotone and pushed him towards sleep again. He realised that he had goose pimples all over his flesh.

Makhanlal picked up a glass of water kept beside his cot and drank a large gulp. Then he lit a cigarette. The room was deliquescing in the sweltering heat after the rain. He found it difficult to breathe and felt heaviness in his chest. He vaguely thought that he should call Lolita before something serious happened. But Makhanlal didn't get much time. Sleep was splashing in, like a mighty ocean, on the banks of his wakefulness. Someone was gently nudging him to sleep. The scooter was going around in his head faster and faster. It occurred to him suddenly that someone had walked ahead of him through his life. Who had kept the cardboard ticket in the weighing machine, waiting for him? Who removed a mask for a brief moment in that unreal restaurant and allowed Makhanlal a glimpse of that hidden fire? The room showed up itself like a convex mirror in another flash of lightning, and on that mirror, Makhanlal saw himself. His chest was like a white wall. As lightning flashed on the wall again, it looked like the chest of god. On it, Makhanlal saw a neat bullet hole. The next moment, the wall cringed in agony and bit its wound.

Where did he drop the cigarette? He could not find it. He made a last, desperate attempt to sit up and call Lolita at the same time. But after sometime, he gave up. Someone was controlling a switch that looked like the reed of a piano and repeatedly flashed lightning. He stretched his arms, searching for the cigarette. It must be lying in some dark corner of this room ... it is burning too. He sensed an acrid smell and the warmth of its light. He was sanguine that it had rolled off to a pile of used clothes, or touched the leg of a wooden chair or even someone's careless hair in a bed and was burning without pity.

'Why this way? Why?' asked Makhanlal. He recalled that for a long while, he had been looking for a burning cigarette in a dark room. He was absolutely sure that the cigarette was burning, he could feel it. He thrashed about in his desperate effort to sit up and call someone.

Makhanlal gives up when a stray dog barks for the first time in the night. He knows he is dying. And dying an inglorious death, like an insect. As blood drips from someone's wound into the eyes, the weighing machine extends an arm like a traffic policeman and hands over a ticket. Makhanlal doesn't see anything. As the last delusion splashes upon him like a wave, he hears indistinctly – Lolita has been calling him.

But by now, Makhanlal is tossing about and drifting farther and farther away from the shores towards high seas.

The Storm

The advertisement shows a girl munching a biscuit, a hint of smile on her face. For a long moment, Bodri looks at the newspaper ad. The newspaper isn't his, it belongs to Pulinbehari, who's sitting beside him. Pulinbehari is fond of reading papers. God knows why! As he fixes his gaze on the paper, Bodri gets the message that he too should eat those biscuits. That's what advertisements are meant to say, aren't they?

As this girl is munching biscuits, you too should eat them. But Bodri cannot quite fathom why he should. He picks up the gamchha, the coarse hand towel, lying on his lap and wipes his brow vigorously. The summer is killing this year. Jackfruits ripen quickly in this heat. The heat is scalding, and it is sultry too. There are not even a few scattered clouds, like ragged torn cloth, to cover the angry face of the sun. The sky looks like a shining, freshly wiped courtyard. If you hit the ground with a shovel now, the sound would be metallic.

The girl with biscuit is seen no more. Pulinbehari has turned the page. Presently, a TV ad stares at Bodri. That too has a wench, leaning on a TV set, smiling. In this world, nothing seems possible without women. A sigh escapes Bodri.

Pulinbehari is sixty-three years of age. Strongly built, his hair is speckled with grey. He is in an unclean dhoti, a sweaty, grubby kurta and spectacles. An influential man. He has been bending down to read a news story. Must be something interesting. Newspapers are like women, backbiting, coming up with all kinds of juicy stories.

Although the train is moving, not much wind is flowing in through the windows. What has been blowing is like the gust from a blacksmith's bellow. Bodri hasn't managed to find a window seat. There are two men between him and the window. And next to him, on the other side, is Pulinbehari: four of them in a seat meant for three. That is the rule. The compartment is tightly packed. There were fans above once upon a time, someone has removed them.

Bodri was not born with a silver spoon. He minds neither heat nor cold. But he is more at home in open spaces, and is not much used to being in a cage.

The train stops in between two stations, as it often does. Pulinbehari has a watch on his left wrist. Glancing at it, he says, 'If we reach by four, we'd be able to catch the last train home.'

'We must go back. I've left the small girl behind.'

'Oho! Why do you worry so much? You haven't left her floating on water. She's with your sister. And Bilasi takes good care of her.'

'If we don't return, she'll cry. She doesn't want to stay with her aunt at night. Besides, Bilasi sleeps like a log, if the child gets scared for some reason and calls her, she won't wake up.'

Looking at his watch once more, Pulin says, 'Four more stations. We'll get off after that. From the station, it's three miles at the most. Looks like we'd be able to make it. The last train is at nine thirty.'

From among those thronging there, someone says, 'Nine twenty. Where are you going?'

'Moulubi Bazaar.'

'Aw! Long way to go.'

Pulin lifts his kurta and scratches his stomach noisily. Sliding on perspiration, his glasses have come down to the tip of his nose. Two of his front teeth are missing. Says he, 'It would be okay if the train isn't delayed any more.'

That is how trains run in this part of the world. They stop, take a rest, and at times, fall asleep. This train shows no signs of moving either.

Bodri feels a little restless. The heat, the sweat or the crowds don't bother him, but the prospect of delay does. If they are late – Bodri has decided – he would take a return train from the station itself. Bilasi wasn't too keen to leave her in-laws' place. She has a large family to look after. She had to be coaxed to come over. She wants to go back tomorrow itself. Bodri's daughter Nandarani is three years of age. Bilasi has three daughters and a son. During the day, Nandarani would have a nice time gambolling with her cousins. But at night, she has to be with her baba. A motherless child, she clings to Bodri. As a father, he has a perception about his daughter, but the daughter too has her own perceptions. It is possible that the daughter is not that worried about her father. What Bodri thinks his daughter thinks about him may not, after all, be true.

'Pulinda, what shall we do?'

Pulin wipes his nose with a dirty handkerchief. Reinstating the glasses to their original perch, he says, 'Why worry so much?' He folds the newspaper and makes a half-hearted attempt to fan himself. For Pulinbehari, returning home is not such a major issue. He may be a headman in the village, but in his large family, nobody cares much for him. His sons have grown up, daughters have been married off, and he himself is away from home most of the time, minding his myriad businesses. He can park himself anywhere he pleases. No one would miss him for a couple of days.

Pulin says, 'Which is more important, finalising the deal or returning back?'

'It's not such a big deal!' Bodri turns his gaze away.

Someone has lit a bidi. The pungent smell is wafting towards them. In an already stuffy compartment, the bidi smoke makes life even more stifling. Around them is a torpid crowd of people. But there is very little noise. The passengers, gasping in the heat, have little energy to talk. Only a few words like bastard, son of a bitch, f... the railways and the like can be heard.

After blowing a tired whistle, the train resumes its journey at last. Looking at his watch, Pulin says, 'We'd be able to make it.'

'Make what?'

'We'll have enough time. Don't worry.'

'Still four stations to go, many things can happen in between.'

Face caustic, Pulin looks out. The sun is real strong today. The fields look like a store of steel utensils.

The next station was not far off. As some people got off, the compartment became a little lighter. The two men sitting next to the window left too, but Bodri doesn't go over to the window seat. The sun is falling there at an angle.

Vendors selling jhalmuri, cucumbers and toothpaste have got off after exhausting themselves. A young tea-seller has boarded the compartment and is shouting now.

Pulin asks, 'Like to have tea?'

'Oh no, not in this heat!'

'Poison kills poison.'

'I don't want. You go ahead.'

Pulin buys himself a cup. As he sips the tea, he says, 'There used to be auto rickshaws earlier. The road is in such a bad shape during the last two years that nothing plies now.'

Bodri knows things are turning for the worse in the country, but it makes little difference to him. He works in the field from early morning to dusk. In order to survive, he has to squeeze himself dry. Things haven't become better or worse for him. He just scrapes through. Only the prospect of drought or flood worries him.

Bodri is a little surprised when scores of people get off at the next station. Pulin says, 'This is the day for the weekly market at Haripur. Besides, there is a fair for the Chaitra Sankranti. The crowd was for Haripur alone, otherwise, this train goes empty.'

Not many passengers are left behind. The unshackled wind seems to blow away the heat to some extent. Pulin has not disposed of his earthen cup. Presently he throws it out of the window and says, 'You are a lucky man, do you understand? You'll see, your fortune will turn the moment the marriage is fixed.'

'I don't see any sign of good fortune. The beginning itself is inauspicious. The way this train is moving, we may have to return from the station itself.'

Pulin ignores him. He says, 'The family are direct descendants of Goddess Katyayani, do you understand? Not a jot of untruth about it. Everyone in the area knows ... A bride comes from Ajapur, only thirteen years of age. She looks like an image of the goddess. The moment she steps into the village, two years of drought ends, it starts pouring. Fruits bloom in trees. Wherever she goes, she leaves behind footmarks of the goddess. One day, there is a mishap as she serves food to her elder brother-in-law. The anchal of her sari slips off her head. Both her hands are engaged, what would she do? Everyone around sees: the bride takes out another pair of arms and covers her head. In the darkness, some people even saw the third eye on her forehead.'

'I've heard that story earlier.'

'Did I tell you this story?'

'Not you. Someone else said something similar about some other bride.'

'Oh no! It's about the same bride. The legend has spread all over. Everyone in this area knows.'

'Even if it is true, it's an old story! Your uncle's daughter is not the same girl.'

'When a goddess comes to a family, the family is blessed. They have a tradition.'

'A long time has passed Pulinda, those traditions are gone.'

'This happened, say, a hundred or hundred and fifty years back. Not very long ago. Say, in my father's time.'

'Agreed. But even that doesn't help much. If the family has such a great tradition, why do they want me as a bridegroom?'

Pulin smiles through his bushy moustache, 'Why not? Are you a bad match? You have fifteen bighas of land, a two-bigha pond, and a garden with so many fruit-bearing trees.'

'Does that make one a good match?'

'What else does one need?'

'Character, education, a decent family tree.'

'What's wrong with your character? As regards education, you know Bangla and can even sign your name in English, not a mean feat. And, as far as ancestry's concerned, you are the grandson of Haradhan Biswas, so there's nothing wrong with that either.'

The train crosses the stations quickly.

Pulin says anxiously, 'Get ready, get ready. The next station; the train is slowing down.'

They get off. Looking at his watch, Pulin gives Bodri a broad smile and says, 'We are not late, it is only five past four. We'll catch the nine thirty train easily.'

'Unless your three miles stretch to five.'

'Oh no! It's certainly not that far.'

The road meanders through a barren field. Although it was not tarred, it was a decent gravelled road once. But being in disrepair for a long time, it is in a bad shape now.

Pulin says, 'The road has been sanctioned. It would be repaired soon. Next year, when you come here on the son-in-law's day, you would smile all the way in an auto, twirling your moustache. Do you understand?'

'You don't even have the eggs. And you have started counting the chickens? I have no desire to tie the knot a second time. I've come only because you forced me. Do you think I'll leave Nandarani to the tender mercies of a stepmother?'

'Okay, okay. First see for yourself. Don't think my uncle is an old man. He is my father's aunt's son, he's my junior by five years. And the girl is his second wife's youngest. She wouldn't be more than fifteen or sixteen.'

Bodri knows these details. Pulin has narrated them not once, but many times over. He has made life miserable for Bodri with his ceaseless pestering. Bodri had to come over with him today only to wriggle out of it. After seeing the girl, he would reject her. He is least interested in marrying again. He has asked Shobha khuri of their village to look after his daughter. When he goes off to the field, the old woman takes care of the child. And when Nandarani grows up a little, say when she is five or so, she would no longer need constant looking after. She would play around with other village girls and grow up on her own, like wild plants do. Bodri would be a free man then. He is on the wrong side of thirty, there is no need for him to marry again.

Pulin talks nonstop as he walks ahead of Bodri.

'The caste matches too. As if god himself has arranged it.'

Bodri doesn't respond. The heat is so intense that he feels parched even if he opens his mouth.

The first village is Gobindopur, the second, Sonadanga; Moulubi Bazaar is the third village along the road. Bodri can estimate the distance. It won't be more than three miles.

Moulubi Bazaar is like an oasis in a desert. It has lots of trees, and doesn't wear a dusty look like the previous villages they crossed.

'Do you know why? There are twenty seven ponds and a lake here. And an irrigation canal too. This is a highly prosperous village. No wonder! Goddess Katyayani herself lived in this village.

Bodri feels a little scared. He is not sure why.

'Are you feeling nervous?'

'No, what's there to be nervous about?'

Bodrinath has to concede, Moulubi Bazaar is prosperous. There are plenty of trees. And ponds in every locality. The village is pretty large, lots of people live here. There is a market place for every day of the week, and on two days, there is a haat where traders come from far and near.

From a distance, Pulin points to him, 'Can you see the Shiva temple there? Their house is just behind it.'

The house is old, but fairly impressive. The floor and walls are cemented and the roof is made of corrugated iron sheets. The courtyard is indeed large and has in it three straw barns. There is a vegetable garden, coconut and areca nut trees.

Pulinbehari yells from the gateway, 'What happened, where've you all gone?'

There was no need for shouting. Two men were chatting in one corner of the veranda. A thin, dark man gets up and says, 'Oh! Bhaipo has come!'

'He's my uncle, understand? His daughter.'

The uncle sports sandalwood paste on his forehead and a neckband made of rudraksh beads around his neck, signs of a religious sect. He is in a dhoti and undershirt. His face betrays cunning. Bodri observes him closely.

Pulin climbs onto the veranda and says, 'We have little time. Have to catch the return train at nine thirty. Do you understand?'

Although the man is an uncle, he is younger than Pulin. So the relationship is rather complex. Uncle Kadam Das says, 'Why should you go back tonight? We have organised a fair for the Chaitra Sankranti, spend a couple of days with us.'

Pulin shakes his head vigorously and says, 'No! I have come only because of this Bodri. He can't stay back, so ....'

So saying, he takes off his kurta. His whole body is covered with festering prickly heat. 'Give me a hand-fan. And a tender coconut,' he says.

Kadam Das goes into the house displaying a sense of urgency. The man who was talking with him now moves forward and says, 'This part of the veranda is in the sun. The other side would be more comfortable.'

Bodri keenly observes this man too. He is young, almost a lad. He is very polite and seems soft natured. Pulin suddenly says, 'Isn't it Ekram?'

'Yes, master.'

'What happened to your court case?'

'Dragging on.'

Pulin has a soft corner for legal matters. He loves litigation. Throwing the kurta on his shoulder, he says, 'Let's go somewhere where we can talk peacefully. Let me listen to the whole story.'

Bodri watches them walking up to the main gate, talking. Their discussion shows no signs of early conclusion. Legal matters are not easily disposed of.

Kadam Das comes out with a boy who looks like a cowherd. The boy has two freshly cut tender coconuts in his hands.

'Please drink the water. Other things are being arranged.'

Taking the coconut, Bodri says, 'Can I have some water please? I'm very thirsty.'

'Yes, of course! Putu, go, fetch water from the well quickly.'

The cowherd runs away.

'Bhaipo! Won't you drink coconut water?'

Pulinbehari raises his hand as if to reassure Kadam Das, without interrupting his conversation with Ekram.

After finishing the coconut, Bodri gulps down the water too. His insides were as dry as a piece of over-burnt brick.

The boy places two iron chairs on the veranda and says, 'Please sit down.' The sun is shut out too by hanging a heavy bedsheet from a string between two posts in the veranda. Hand fans are supplied.

But Pulinbehari proves to be a difficult customer. The discussion drags on and on. He walks off to a still more secluded place with Ekram, and then still further away. After a while, they are no longer seen.

Kadam Das had perhaps gone in to inform about their arrival. Bodri suddenly noticed, a crowd of women were jostling at the main door leading to the house. There were a few kids too. Bodri had had a shave that morning, and had trimmed his moustache. He was wearing a green kurta over a handloom dhoti. Although a little soggy in sweat, his dress was quite natty. He didn't turn around again. Fanning himself with a palm frond fan, he cursed the irresponsible Pulinbehari and his late forefathers. The fellow had deserted Bodri at his hour of peril. If he had any sense of responsibility! Should he have left Bodri alone in such an embarrassing situation?

The cowherd places a stool before Bodri in anticipation. A scraggy old man takes his seat thereon. His moustache was grey, and complexion copper brown; he was in an undershirt and dhoti. A gurgling noise came out of his throat as he spoke – probably because of phlegm – and he smiled courteously. 'Baba, I've heard a lot about you from Kadam.'

Bodri doesn't know how to respond to such gambits. He was married only once in the past. And on that occasion, he did not have to go through the hassle of approving the prospective bride. His aunt had fixed the match. On the appointed day, he returned from the fields a little early and left with the groom's party. His wife was from a nearby village. The marriage was performed with the accompaniment of noisy cymbals. There was no problem. They lived happily for five years. About a year and a half ago, Basanti was afflicted with an illness that could not be diagnosed. She had acute bouts of stomach ache and passed out from time to time. A doctor checked her and prescribed medicines. When her condition became worse, she was taken to a hospital in town. The doctor there said, it was too late, the appendix had 'burst'. Otherwise, Bodri would not have been here in this sweaty afternoon.

The old man heaves a sigh and says, 'Wherever girls from this family go, prosperity is showered from the heavens, do you understand? It has to be, Goddess Katyayani herself came to this family. It was at the time of my great-grandfather. Do you understand? He was a tough man, but he was deeply religious too. So, my great-grandmother came. Her name was Katyayani and she indeed was an embodiment of Goddess Katyayani ....'

'Yes, I have heard the story.'

'Of course, of course! Everyone knows. How many children do you have?'

'Only one daughter. Three years old.'

'She will be in safe hands. She would never know that she's with a stepmother.'

Bodri has been perspiring profusely. A few more women and children have come and joined the group around him. Among them is a gigantic woman who looks rather overbearing. An embarrassed Bodri cannot raise his eyes. More importantly, the crowd has blocked whatever breeze that was floating in. It is stifling in the veranda.

The overbearing woman suddenly says, 'There, Khublo, why don't you fan him? He has come all the way. He's feeling hot.'

Khublo is a boy of about fifteen years. He takes the fan from Bodri and starts fanning him. In his enthusiasm, he hits Bodri a couple of times with the fan. Bodri lowers his head slightly to dodge it. He cannot figure out who is who in the family. Not that it matters. His sole aim is to catch the train at nine thirty. Would the girl manage without her father at night?

The situation is messy. He has come to see a prospective bride, but instead, everybody is gaping at him. Bodri cannot lift his head. He can see the forearms of the gigantic woman. She has steel and conch bangles on her wrist. That means she is married. Whose wife is she?

Kadam Das comes back hurriedly and says to the woman, 'Are you through? They have to return by the night train!'

The gigantic woman says, 'So what? There's plenty of time.'

'It's past six.'

Bodri does not have a watch on him. He feels a little apprehensive when he hears it is already past six. They would have to walk three miles in the dark. They would be lucky to catch the train. He hates the way Pulinbehari has been behaving. He can afford to stay back, but Bodri cannot.

From behind the crowd of bystanders, a pair of dark and thin hands with bangles is thrust forward. They carry a bell metal plate overflowing with sweets. And a glass of water.

'Please eat, baba.'

He is hungry, and takes the plate. But how does one eat in front of so many prying eyes? The situation is indeed difficult. So he says, 'Let Pulinda come.'

Kadam says with a sense of urgency, 'Yes, of course, where is bhaipo? Putu! Putu! please go to the road and see. He has no sense. Please ask him to come.'

The boy named Putu sprints away.

Bodri continues sitting, saying nothing. He is perspiring despite the fanning. His gamchha is in the bag, but he cannot take it out in the presence of so many people. It would look odd.

Pulin didn't go very far. He returns shortly. As he pushes open the gate and enters the compound, he says, 'Listen to me. No one wins a court case by trusting the lawyer blindly. The main thing is how *you* follow up. What does the lawyer do? He takes his fees and talks, that's all. You have to give him the points.'

Pulin makes his way through the crowd and gets onto the veranda with an air of importance. He says, 'What nonsense! Is this a circus? Move away, move away, let there be a little breeze.'

He too is handed over a plate with sweets. As he eats, he says, 'I brought a few points to Ekram's notice. He's very happy.'

As soon as they finish eating, Kadam says, 'Please come in. It would be a little hot inside, but the girl can't be shown in the veranda.'

Pulin says, 'As if it is cooler outside! Come in, Bodri! Don't worry, you'll catch the nine thirty train.'

Within the room, the light was hazy and confusing. The doors and windows were not big. Besides, there was a big leafy tree right outside a window. In one corner of the room was a cot covered with a sheet. At the foot of the cot, there was a big pile of trunks and boxes on a bench.

In one side of the room was a wooden chair. There was nothing facing it. The cowherd Putu brings in the two iron chairs from the veranda and places them in front. A fair number of people are crowding the room. As soon as Bodri and Pulin take their seats, Khublo starts fanning them from behind. Pulin says, 'Faster, son, faster; we're bathing in sweat. Who will bring the girl? Please bring her. After all, she's going to a middle class family. There's no need to deck her up.'

There is a little jostling at the door leading to the inner part of the house. The girl is coming. Bodri feels a little nervous. He hopes the girl doesn't have four arms!

He cannot look at the person who was being pushed through the crowd. Instead, he watches a framed picture of a bird on the wall. A yellow bird. He doesn't have the faintest idea which bird it could be. It is a piece of needlecraft.

'Look up, look at her. See how she is. Why are you looking the other way?'

Bodri first lowers his head before looking up. All the faces in the room were a uniform shade of darkness. He was sitting outside, he is yet to adjust to the dim light within.

Even then, a pair of eyes catches his attention. A pair? Or a triad? Does the girl have three eyes? Given the yarns spun by Pulin, he wouldn't be surprised!

But it is not so. The confusion was caused by the longish bindi she was wearing on her forehead. He cannot figure out much about her looks, and it does not matter either. On the way back, he would tell Pulin that he didn't like her.

Suddenly, a gust of cold wind blew in from nowhere. Today, Bodri's mind is cluttered with all sorts of eerie thoughts. The wind startles him. How could there be a gust of cold air?

Someone says in a deep rustic voice, 'A storm is brewing!'

Before the sentence was completed, there was a thunderclap like a lion's roar. Finished. Bodri had no inkling of the storm. Of course, he was in no position to notice the clouds building up, surrounded as he was by people.

Pulinbehari is chewing paan. How did he get one? After all, this is his uncle's house, someone might have given him. He says, 'Thank God! Let there be a storm. I would get rid of my prickly heat.'

Some men and women dart out of the room. A few things have to be taken care of in the household before the storm strikes.

The gigantic woman says, 'Oh! Katyayani, why are you bowing down? Raise your head. Let him see you properly. How else can he take a liking to you?'

The pleasant wind doesn't stop. On the contrary, it becomes stronger. Bodri, like any other farmer, knows how quickly a northwester develops in early summer. It comes in without warning. There would be a couple of thunderclaps, and bags of dust would start swirling in the wind. Doors and windows were being closed in a hurry. There was a minor pandemonium.

Pulin says, 'Let there be, let there be a little wind. You have blocked every pore.'

As a matter of fact, when all the doors and windows were closed, the room became utterly dark. A strong gust of wind blew over the tin roof, making a loud clatter. The next gust shook the door violently. Then the world trembled with a crashing roar of thunder. In the courtyard, people and animals were running helter-skelter. Doors and windows were closing with loud bangs.

In that raging storm, the people within the room fall silent. From close quarters, there is a deafening thunderclap.

The squall doesn't scare Bodri. Every year, he comes across such thunderstorms in open fields. Sitting in his chair, he tries to figure out how bad the storm was. If it continued, he would miss the train.

Suddenly, for the second time, Bodri has the delusion! He clearly sees not two, but three eyes shining steadily like the light of earthen lamps in the darkness. One vertical eye in between two normal ones.

Bodri is convinced that he has lost his head. There is nothing. The room is dark, just as it was a little earlier. Pulin lights the torch to dispel the darkness. The girl's chair is empty. She has left at some point. The crowd has thinned too. Only the old man, the gigantic woman and Kadam Das are in the room.

Pulin says, 'We are in for trouble. How will we go?'

'It won't continue for more than ten minutes,' Bodri says, 'it will stop.'

'Yes it will stop, but have you thought about how the roads will be like?'

Bodri smiles faintly. He is a farmer, used to mud and slush. He feels pity for villagers who speak like urban babus.

The storm becomes stronger, although it hasn't started raining yet.

Kadam Das says, 'All the mango flowers are gone.'

Pulin says, 'Let them go, but let it turn a little cooler. Cultivation has almost come to a standstill!'

'That's true.'

The sprightly storm was almost tearing away the roofing sheets. Kadam Das looks upward. There was a loft underneath the roof. And there were lots of things on it.

Although the roof over this cottage survives, somewhere in the distance, there was the sound of a tin roof being ripped apart. It crashed on the ground with a hideous noise. There were two consecutive sounds of trees being snapped.

Kadam Das says with a sour face, 'An areca nut tree is gone, and the jaam tree.'

Switching off the torch, Pulin says, 'Aw Bodri!'

Bodri says, 'Please see the time, Pulinda.'

'Six thirty two. But what's the point of seeing the time? We can't start until the wind drops.'

After this, there is silence for some more time. And then, it starts raining. At first, a few large drops, making a clatter on the roof. Then pouring rain. And later, a deluge.

Bodri sits quietly. He thinks neither about the rains, nor about the last train, nor about his daughter. He has been thinking, was it a figment of his imagination? What did he see? Katyayani's tale is a mere yarn. Stories do spread like that. Why, then, did he see what he saw?

Suddenly, the old man says, 'It's a good omen.'

'What's a good omen?' asks Pulin.

'This nor'wester.'

'Aw.'

Kadam heaves a sigh, 'Anyway, the danger is past. The roof over the cowshed has blown away. It isn't much.'

Bodri has been sitting quietly. He no longer seems to be in a hurry. He may go, or he may stay back. It is Pulin who reminds him, 'Get up, it is almost seven.'

The storm is over. The rain too has almost stopped. There is only a gentle pitter-patter on the roof now. Bodri gets up.

Kadam opens the door for them and says, 'So you are going? I am sorry, it was such a bother for you. And you'll have still more trouble going back, on the slushy road ….'

Bodri says, 'No problem.'

As soon as he steps on the veranda, he realises, there was a big mess in front of them, in that darkness. Lots of trees have fallen, branches have snapped, many roofs have been blown away. They hear people shouting, there is terror in their voice.

Two men are crossing a field enveloped by vast darkness in the light of a torch. A wet breeze has been blowing softly. The path is slushy and slippery.

'Bodri, say something.'

'What do you want me to say?'

'Did you like her?'

After a long moment, Bodri says, 'Do I have a choice?'

The Golden Horse

Three rabbits rummage through the groundnut field, upturn chunks of earth and ferret out groundnuts. They hold the nuts with their forepaws and chew them merrily. Their ears flap in happiness.

Mysterious shadows dance within the maize field. From inside comes a sibilant sound. Two children tear off tender corncobs, peel them and dig their teeth into the soft pods. Corn milk bursts out of the pods. Their mouths fill with tasty juice, they suck it. They look at each other and exchange meaningful smiles. The girl's hair is dry and unkempt, her thick lips do not hide a bucktooth. The boy is naked but for a dirty loincloth, a tuft of long hair hangs behind his shaved head.

The girl's father has removed weeds from under the plants, and has gathered a pile of them in one corner of the garden. Here, dry leaves fall through the day. He has made a heap out of fallen leaves, twigs and a weaverbird's nest that has fallen off a silk cotton tree. He carefully lights a bidi with a matchstick and lights the weaverbird's nest with it. The heap catches fire. He smells the sweet, pungent smell of burning leaves. Sitting down on the grass a little away, he smokes absently.

From within the maize field, the girl smells the heady scent. Bapu is burning dry leaves. She tears off two corncobs and ties them in her sari; she would roast the corn. And then she notices the rabbits. They are uprooting groundnut plants.

Turning around, she calls the boy, 'Ei Genia, they are eating groundnuts.'

'Who?'

'See there.'

Genia is the son of the blind beggar Surdas Ramji. Genia always has a short stick in his hand. He holds one end of it and his father holds the other. Holding the stick that way, he leads his father on the roads, from house to house, for begging. They board the shuttle train to Joshidih, or even a mail train, and go all the way to Jhajha or Madhupur. The boy now jumps out with the same stick in his hand.

Three rabbits scamper away, but don't go far. They cross the boundary of this garden, passing under a barbed wire fence and enter the garden on their north. In order to impress the girl, Genia jumps a couple of times with his stick, shouts. The free end of his loincloth always hangs between his legs. As he jumps, this end swings like a tail. Seeing it, the girl bursts into laughter.

They cross the groundnut field and go around the massive, silent bungalow to reach the fire. Sitting away from the heat of the fire, Bhootnath absently holds a bidi between his muddy fingers. His gaze is fixed at nowhere. The girl has seen her bapu sitting like that ever since her birth. She knows, he doesn't like the soil of this place. He lived in a land where the earth was richer and the plants much more green, lush and colourful. That place had plenty of water too. The borderline between land and water was often smudged there. Here, it is different. In that place called Dhaka, Bapu had a wife and son too. Both of them died, during a riot, trapped inside their burning house. Bapu alone managed to escape and flee to Calcutta. The Saha babus too were from the same place, and hired him as an assistant. On noticing the man's love for trees and plants, the old master said, 'There is no one in our house in Baidyanath Dham. The gardener has become old and infirm. You better go and work there. You have a way with plants. Go and look after the garden there.'

The old Bihari gardener lost his job. Bhootnath felt sorry for him. And out of his sorrow grew his desire to kill two birds with one stone. The old man had a daughter. She was not a Bengali, but had the quiet charm of the Bihar countryside. Bhootnath decided to free the old man from the shackles of the daughter; he himself had not become too old for marriage then. And he wanted to bury the sadness that gnawed at his mind all the time. The old man mumbled, 'My daughter's like a milch cow. You can marry her, but you've to pay two hundred rupees, in cash.' Bhootnath was stunned. He had reckoned he was doing the old man a favour by agreeing to marry his daughter without asking for dowry, but the old man was demanding a price! But that is the custom here. They settled for one hundred. That too, not in one go, but in four instalments. Bhootnath set up his home in the outhouse of the Saha babus' bungalow, with his wife acquired over four instalments. There was plenty of land around them. He happily immersed himself in the garden. Fruits and flowers bloomed. And Kamli blossomed in Etwari's arms.

That Kamli is now carefully extending her slender hand towards the burning leaves to roast an ear of corn; the beggar's son Genia is behind her. Bhootnath observes the scene with detachment. He has got another wife, another offspring; once again he has been enjoying the proximity of earth. Yet, for some reason, he has become permanently absentminded. At times, he feels he is not really tied to this world. The bond is tenuous, it might snap any moment. And the thought makes him sit down under the shades of trees and ponder. He thinks of water, of the variegated colours of soils; and at times, of his lost wife and son and the scarlet skies of disaster. Or perhaps, he doesn't think of his past, only an agony keeps him separated from others, like a solitary crane in the sky. After sitting still and unthinking for some time, he suddenly realises that the fish of thoughts that created ripples upon the surface of the water, has dived below. It can no longer be caught. The game keeps him motionless for hours. The light of his bidi dies and it tastes bitter. At such times, if Kamli comes in and calls him bapu, he gets up with a start and thinks: Who is this girl?

As she bites the corn, her body soaks in the taste of roasted corn. Looking at her, Genia smiles, and she smiles back.

The boy says in a small voice, 'A little salt …'

Kamli notices a gnat climbing up her father's back. She gets up in a flash and throws off the fly with a swish of her sari-end.

Looking up, her father says, 'What was it?'

'A gnat.'

Bapu falls silent again. Lights another bidi.

'Bapu, that crazy doctor's rabbits come every day and destroy our groundnut plants.'

'Chase them away.'

'Don't I? But I must have a dog. Let Genia's Chameli have a litter, then. You agree Bapu, don't you?'

'All right.'

Bapu is sweet, but Ma hates dogs.

The large garden has been luxuriating in the sun and the wind. Insects are flying back after pollinating the flowers. The sound of flying insects ... Genia jumps over flowerbeds, Kamli following him. Time and again, they look at the silent magnificent bungalow, and colourful dreams cross their minds.

Opening a grille gate, the two of them enter the veranda of the building. On one side of the veranda is a row of rooms. Large padlocks hang on their doors. They have seen it many a time, but once again, they lift the slats of the windows and peep inside. Within the rooms, there is more darkness than light. Still, they can see the gorgeous furniture. A large ornate bed, a dressing table, flower vases, framed pictures on the walls, glass cases full of toys, bookshelves. The children go around and gape at them by lifting the window slats of different rooms. Every fifteen days, Bhootnath unlocks these rooms and Etwari goes in with buckets of water and a broomstick. The rooms are washed. At those times, Kamli enters the rooms and touches various objects. But Etwari doesn't allow Genia to go in. She says, 'He is a thief! He'll remove things and vanish in a trice.'

So Genia observes the contents with thirsty eyes. Every day.

But Kamli does not allow him the pleasure for long. Greed is written all over his face. She pulls down the slats and says, 'Enough!'

Genia says with a smile, 'There is a golden horse in the glass case, isn't there?'

Kamli pouts. 'Maybe. There are so many things,' she says.

In a window facing north, a bar is missing. Genia has noticed it.

Blind Ramji sleeps through the morning. Does one's body become cold with age? He loves the warmth of his bed. He has spread straw on a bamboo platform and over the straw, endless scraps of grimy cloth. That is all he has for a bed, but it gives him warmth! At night, Genia sleeps beside him. He loves the warmth of his son's body. The boy has gone away at the crack of dawn, leaving him behind.

Although his eyes have turned into stone, Ramji can guess the time. His stomach is wrenched by hunger. But he often goes hungry, and is not upset about it. He sits up on the bed slowly, and as he gets off the platform, he calls Genia. His voice is harsh, but affectionate.

Genia does not respond. Ramji goes behind the hut and pees under a bush. Returning to his shack, he drinks water. In two earthen pots, there is rice soaked in water. After eating the rice, he would go out begging, with Genia.

He calls his son a few more times, but no one answers. On removing the lids of the earthen pots, he discovers that the son of a bitch has eaten the rice to the last grain. Nothing has been left behind for the old father.

'Genia-a-a, you son of a bitch!'

Sitting in the sun, Surdas Ramji curses his son in desperation.

In this house, water flows out of the taps like a swift snake. It's sweet too. Kneeling down, Genia drinks it with his cupped hands. A little away, on the cemented base of a water tank, Kamli sits, her face absorbed, serious, as she digs through her hair in search of lice.

Genia is filled with water. But still, as he enjoys the flowing water, he keeps his head buried in the cup of his hands and lets the water flow.

Kamli comes up, and turning off the tap, says, 'Is water available for free? Get lost.'

In front of the outhouse is a spinach field, where Etwari has been plucking spinach stems tenderly. From there, she observes her daughter with the sneak thief son of the blind beggar Surdas. The girl has no sense! She calls, 'Kamli, Eh Kamli!'

The moment Kamli leaves, Genia sprints into the maize field. He breaks off nine or ten cobs. Holding them close to his chest, he furtively runs towards the north. There is a breach in the barbed wire fence. He slips through it and goes over to the main road.

As soon as he hears Genia's footfalls, Ramji stealthily stretches towards his stick.

'Have you come?'

Genia does not respond. But Ramji can guess his position. Suddenly, without warning, he picks up the stick and strikes out, with all his strength.

But Genia is prepared. He skips aside, like a rabbit. A few corncobs fall off his chest. The stick hits the ground with a thud.

'Aren't you ashamed, you son of a whore? Haven't left even one grain of rice for your blind bapu?'

From a safe distance, Genia throws a corncob at his father. At first, Surdas shouts, 'You are hitting me, you little mouse, you are hitting your old, blind bapu?'

As he tries to pick up the stick, he feels the corncob. He picks it up and tenderly touches the peas after peeling it. Then he smiles.

'Where did you get it? In Bhootua's garden? Will you roast it? Please light a fire.'

Genia does not reply. Entering the shack silently, he puts on his dirty, torn canvas cap and comes out.

His father, beggar Surdas Ramji sits in the sun with his lightless eyes and nibbles at the corn. The skin on his face, as also the rest of his body, is chapped, his hair is unkempt and he has a rough beard over broken cheeks. Clothed in a grimy loincloth, he looks a lunatic. But Genia does not notice anything abnormal about his father's appearance.

He offers the short stick to Surdas and says, 'Let's go.'

Surdas Ramji runs his hand in the air and catches hold of the stick.

The time isn't right for begging. Most of the houses in this pilgrim town are unoccupied. This is not the season for pilgrimage and the place is almost deserted. They trudge through the forlorn town, each holding an end of the stick. Chameli walks by their side, rubbing her coat on their bare legs.

'Do you meet that whore?'

'No!'

'No! Do you think I don't understand because I can't see? I know that you go to see her.'

'When do I go?'

'Everyday. When I call you, at times, I don't find you. You go there to stuff yourself. When you sleep, I feel your stomach. It's often full. Where do you get so much food?'

'No, promise.'

'Promise upon whom?'

'Upon Baidyanathji!'

Surdas falls silent. The whore has left him and is living with Mahindar, on the other side of the railway track for the last four years. She left her only son behind, but the boy craves for his mother. He is the only support Surdas has; if he too goes away, the old man would be finished. So he's careful.

'Don't you ever go to her. Don't worry, I'll feed you. I have money.'

'Yes, I know.'

Ramji's ears prick up like a rabbit's. He says sharply, 'What do you know?'

'About your money.'

Ramji is gripped by a new anxiety. Does he know? Does he really know?

He walks absently.

Suddenly he says, 'Walk faster, the train ....'

'Where?'

'The ground is shaking, don't you feel it?'

Genia doesn't, but his blind father does.

It is better to have a husband who quarrels, who is a wife-beater rather than one who is unconcerned. Etwari took some time to realise that her husband Bhootnath was detached, indifferent. There was a time when she used to draw delicate designs on her palms with mehendi, when she used to put a colourful bindi on her forehead or put kajal on her eyes. But even those days, Bhootnath hardly noticed her. Etwari reckoned he did not care much for the Bihari beauty aids and decided to paint her feet with aalta, put dollops of sindoor on the parting of her hair and wear the sari the Bengali way. And then, she resigned herself to the fact that her man cared for no such thing. All that mattered to him was working the soil, and at times, sitting down as if he was under a spell. Etwari used to feel awful. But of late, she doesn't. It is not that she doesn't enjoy a good fight. But with this man, she doesn't argue at all. Bhootnath is much older than she is. Already, he has streaks of grey. And because he thinks all the time, he looks glum, much older than his age. All this makes Etwari somewhat respectful towards her husband. Besides, the man is from another part of the country.

Having had his afternoon meal, the man is smoking a bidi sitting on a charpai in front of the outhouse, wearing the same distant look. When Etwari comes out to wash the plates, she looks at him for a fleeting second. She likes watching him. Soon, Kamli would finish her meal and come out to massage her father's arms and legs. And then, she would tell him many tales. In between the stories, she would bury her face in her father's chest and fall asleep. A dappled shadow of the peepul tree would gently sway over them.

After seeing off the father and son duo at the railway station, Chameli totters back to their shack. On the way, she stops and sniffs the air, and goes this way and that. Wherever she might go, in the afternoon, she would invariably come and stand in the square in front of Kamlis' house. She barks to announce her arrival. And the girl is ready too, she doesn't eat the last few balls of rice. She runs out with the rice in her hand. Chameli wags her tail so wildly that the happy tail runs the risk of dropping off. She is Genia's dog, but hardly anything is left when the beggar and his son finish eating. And Chameli is perpetually hungry. She has to visit Kamli on almost all days. She suffers much ignominy for the sake of a handful of rice. Kamli combs her coat, grinds mehendi leaves to paint designs on her back and pulls the skin on her neck.

A broken earthen plate was lying in the garbage dump. Pouring the rice on that, Kamli talks to Chameli, 'Where has your master gone? For doing business?'

No one shows pity to a blind man without any talent. He could do better business had he been a singer.

Genia tells that to Ramji. But Surdas Ramji has no feel for music. And has a raven's voice.

'You learn, Genia. Learn a few songs from Hindi films.'

Genia feels embarrassed. But he sings when he is alone. At least, he tries. Joshidih's Bhikhan earns a tidy sum by singing in trains to the accompaniment of two small flat stones strapped to his fingers. Genia too has collected two stones.

In the evening, the father and son duo return, boarding a train from Seetarampur or Jhajha. Genia leaves his father alone when they are near the shack. He turns around and starts walking briskly. His father calls out desperately, yells at him, curses him, begs, but Genia doesn't turn around. He runs all the way to the other side of the railway line, to a barrack-like house behind the station building. Every evening, Mahindar, the man with whom his mother lives nowadays, sings. He has an old harmonium. He sits comfortably on a charpai, stretches one leg to bellow the harmonium with the heel and presses the reeds with both hands. He sings with a full-throated voice. Two of his golden teeth glimmer. He is a stylish man. Genia sits in front of him just like Chameli. He listens to the songs with rapt attention and tries to pick up the tunes.

His mother has two more babies now, who crawl around the house like worms and cry loudly. Slowly, the evening turns to night. Most of the days, Ma cooks potato curry with onions and garlic and feeds Genia along with the other kids. As she serves rice, she says, 'I forbid you. You must not start begging like that old scamp.'

Genia smiles, 'But begging is good business if one can sing.'

'Let it be. You don't have to be a beggar. I'll bring you here when the old man dies.'

The promise is not to be taken seriously; Genia knows. After all, his mother lives with another man. Mahindar has two buffaloes and runs a teashop under a banyan tree. His shop is a hangout of petty criminals. He has a quick temper. At times, he beats mother mercilessly. He spits on his toes and makes her lick the slobber. Some evenings, he ties her up before leaving the house. Many a time, Genia has run away in terror on seeing her … the blood dripping from her lips having dried, her eyes swollen, she sits helplessly with her hands and feet tied up behind her back. And the two babies suckling at her breasts even in that condition. Compared to that, Genia is better off with his blind father, although the old man is irritable and no one knows where he hides his savings. But still, Genia is confident. Some day, he would discover the old man's treasure. After he dies, Genia would pull their hut down, dig up the ground, cut up every bamboo post to see if anything is hidden inside. It is certainly there. And with that money, he would take a decent room on rent, buy a harmonium, hang it around his neck and do a roaring business in trains.

Genia returns late. Suddenly, a pale white moon sprinkles milk all over the place and wipes out the miseries of the world. Milk drips down the sparkling white trunk of a eucalyptus tree. Fragrance of flowers fills the sky. In the desolate road, Genia stops, forgetting everything. And then he starts singing in an unrestrained voice overflowing with joy. He dances around, picks up two small stones and plays them like a tambourine.

Genia moves ahead and reaches Kamli's place. An electric bulb is glowing in their house. The main building is enveloped in shadows. But he can see it through the large trees in the garden. The gate is locked. Stillness hangs on the world. In that tranquillity, a golden horse jumps down from the sky before Genia. In a moonlight tastier than fresh milk, he looks at the horse with his mind's eye. Gold means a lot of money. He knows.

His mother left his father behind because of poverty, but hasn't been able to go far. She is on the other side of the railway track and survives despite Mahindar's torture. If Genia finds the golden horse, he would knock down their shack and construct a brick-and-mortar house in its place. He would bring mother back from that ill-tempered Mahindar. Surdas Ramji would warm himself in the winter by wrapping a Bhagalpur shawl and enjoy the sun in their courtyard. And Genia would go all the way to Giridih, crossing Jhajha and Madhupur in an express train, with a harmonium slung around his neck.

He jumps over the gate without making a noise. The trees and bushes have submerged in the transparent milk, casting mysterious shadows. And among them, his shadow looks like a slithering naked man. Through the garden, he moves silently towards the dark patch beside the bungalow. He looks around furtively: nothing is moving.

He stands before the window facing north. One of its bars is missing. He cautiously pulls the shutter; it is bolted from inside. Though closed, it is not secured very tightly. It can be moved. Pushing back one shutter, Genia tries to pull out the other, opening a one-inch gap in between. He pushes the tender fingers of his left hand through the gap and fixes his palm within. He pulls the shutter with all his strength and desperately tries to put his arm in. The two heavy shutters bite into his flesh. The round head of the bolt touches his hand, but he is in no position to hold it. Besides, as he has been pulling the shutter out, the bolt has got stuck more tightly in its groove. Yet, he keeps trying. Like a monster, the two heavy shutters start chewing his hands gleefully. He groans in pain.

A dog has been barking nearby. Genia cannot make out why the wretched creatures bark all the time. He pulls out his hand and loses some skin in the process. It burns. In the moonlight, he searches for a stick or piece of wood in the garden. And gets one too. A small piece of wood that can be used as a wedge. He pulls the shutters apart and sticks in the wedge. And then he puts in his hand once again. With much effort, he can ultimately push his entire hand in.

The dog's bark is coming closer. Far away, he hears Kamli shouting, 'Chameli! Eh Chameli-i-i!'

The dog is none other than Chameli! Bloody whore. The greedy dog comes here twice a day to eat.

Genia concentrates in catching hold of the head of the bolt. And manages to hold it too. And at that time, Chameli comes bounding in through trees and bushes. Barking twice with unexpected pleasure, she whines and rubs her head between Genia's legs, wagging her tail vigorously. She jumps on Genia and licks him.

'Bloody whore!' Genia abuses her, voice muted. And then he lands a solid kick. Chameli rolls over with a yelp. The next moment, she forgets her humiliation and comes forward whining, and continues to express her affection. On the other side, the bolt has been turning loose in his hand. Sweat is pouring out from every pore of his body.

Kamli is coming, holding a kerosene lamp in her hand. She is calling, 'Chameli! Eh Chameli-i-i!'

The bolt is moving, moving. The golden horse jumps. It gallops around in the room, trying to find a way out. Genia's hands are burning, the bones are about to snap, he's turning blue with pain. The window is biting into his arm, gnashing its teeth.

Carrying a smoky lamp, Kamli is coming closer, calling, 'Chameli-i-i!'

Standing between Genia's legs, Chameli is cheerfully responding to the call, 'Wow! Wow!'

The bolt comes out of the clasp and the window opens wide. Genia's numb hand drops down. He holds his limp hand with the other and kicks Chameli once again in the stomach.

In a flash, Genia goes in and closes the shutter behind him. Outside, Chameli looks at the window and barks loudly. Holding the lamp above her head, Kamli observes the scene. She is scared.

The next moment, she turns around and starts running, shouting for her parents.

In the darkness, Genia moves from one room to another. He runs his hand over a door, feels for the bolts and enters the next room. He dashes against furniture and stumbles on doormats and rolled-up carpets. He can't find his bearings in the dark, but desperately tries to reach the room with the glass case and the golden horse. He loses his way, searching for the room. After crossing two rooms, he is flummoxed when he tries to enter the next. That room was bolted from the inside! He understands this truth by running his hand on the door. He reckons this was the central room. And the glass case was in this very room. He furiously pulls at the doorknob. The heavy door is as unmoved as a rock. He tries for quite some time. By then he is tired and exhausted.

He walks in the darkness, aimlessly. Dashes against things, trips and falls. Moves again. Rats run on the floor. He hears the whirr of cockroaches. The known house suddenly seems terribly unknown. He tries all the windows, but cannot find the one with the missing bar. Outside, Chameli has stopped barking. The place has fallen absolutely silent. What will Genia do now? He may be a thief, a beggar and the son of a slut, but he is not above fear. Kamli has gone to fetch people. And, he has lost his way in total darkness. On the other side of a closed door – he knows it for a fact – the golden horse is galloping around, it cannot find its way out either.

Bhootnath has a lighted torch in his hand, Kamli carries a kerosene lamp. They go around the building and pull at each shutter. Everything is in place. Bhootnath says in a detached voice, 'There's nothing wrong. You must have made a mistake.'

They go to sleep, without anxiety.

Late in the night, in his sleep, Surdas Ramji feels cold. Tonight, the bed lacks warmth. He grumbles about it and shivers. He gropes around for Genia. He is the blind man's only support. When he embraces the child, he feels warmth. But tonight, there is no one with him. Is the boy working as a thief's apprentice? Or, did that whore coax him to stay back? Oh God! If that happens, Surdas would be finished, looking and searching for things. He frets, abuses Genia in his sleep. And then, drifts off into deep slumber once again.

Outside, a river of moonlight flows through their courtyard. Chameli observes the scene, half asleep. She barks once or twice. And then, she too curls up and sleeps.

Sometime ago, a naked Genia has fallen asleep in a soft bed upon an ornate cot. Exhausted. He cried. The tears have dried on his cheeks. A couple of drops are still holding on to the corners of his eyes.

In the middle of the night, the shadows are bending and dissolving in the garden. The moonlight is brighter now, a heady scent of flowers has slowed down the breeze.

God has come out in search of dreams for the wretched of the earth. He searches every corner and nets dreams from vast expanses with the effortless ease of an expert fisherman. Then he sprinkles a handful of them. The dreams fall from the sky like radiant stardust under a splendid moon.

Genia is riding a golden horse towards the stars. Behind him is his blind father, and holding on to his waist, his mother. Genia has a stone tambourine in his hand. And playing the instrument, he sings beautifully. Before them lies a golden river. There is no sorrow on the other side of the river. Lots of alms are available there.

Despite the tears in his eyes, Genia smiles in his sleep.

Tomorrow, I Promise ...

He broke the matchstick into two and picked his teeth with the bottom half a long while ago. Now, when he wants to light a bidi, Santulal notices the lone broken matchstick lying in the matchbox pompously, as if to remind him it is his last resort.

A strong wind is blowing today, as it often does in the month of Chaitra. Yesterday, there were a few drops of rain, but today, the sun is blazing away and the wind is dry as a twig. The wretched wind will snuff out the feeble matchstick with a swipe of its paw. And if that happens, Santulal would have to walk two miles without smoking a bidi. After that, he could light one from the ever-lit coir rope at Hajari's shop. But how can anybody walk that long a distance without a smoke? His mouth would salivate, his heart would be lonesome and he would feel he was missing something vital.

Santulal shakes the matchbox. The lone matchstick rattles proudly. Santulal cannot read the mind of the stick. Would or would not the bastard ditch him by burning out just as he was about to light the bidi?

Santulal's hands are not clean. If he jotted down his sins on paper, they would indeed make a long list. One needn't go very far. Even this matchbox – he nipped it when he found it lying in his master's courtyard. The maid had left it behind after lighting a unun, a portable oven, in the open. Later, she came back in search of the matchbox and, not finding it, heaped colourful abuses upon the thief and his forefathers. Although she didn't take names, it was obvious that her target was Santu. Hearing her, he thought: Well, I'll become a good person from tomorrow!

Matchbox in hand, Santu sits down on a mound in the middle of the field. A bidi is clamped between his teeth, but he hasn't tried to light it. He wonders if it was proper for the maid, Saraswati, to abuse his ancestors in such filthy language. More importantly, she cursed his son. After all, she is none other than his wife. It is another matter that these days she lives with a moneyed man. And for that matter, Sukhchandra isn't exactly rolling in wealth either. Of late, after setting up a wheat grinding mill, he thinks he has become a big shot. Not to forget, he has to pay for the upkeep of his first wife too. Saraswati thinks Sukhchandra will treat her like a queen for all time to come. Hah! He is getting ready to kick her out. It won't take all that long.

It was not right of Saraswati to ask his son to go to hell. The son does not belong to Santu alone, he is Saraswati's too. But when she is angry, she doesn't care for such fine distinctions. When in a fit of temper, she loses her head, completely.

On the mound, there are some bald patches of burnt-out grass. Here and there lie pieces of half-burnt wood. That rogue of a sadhu had pitched camp here until recently.

For some time, Santulal has been longing to unburden himself to someone. He has a basketful of woes. One evening, when he heard of the sadhu, he came down to meet him. The sadhu was reputed to be bad tempered. When infuriated, he apparently chased people with burning embers held with a tong. But everyone respects bad tempered, foul-mouthed sadhus, and Santu is no exception.

As Santulal climbed up the mound in the fading light of the evening, he saw the sadhu, hair matted, clothed in nothing but a loincloth, eating something. There was no one around except Motilal of Belpukur, who was cringing like a thief in one corner, holding an open umbrella. Last year, Motilal suffered a big loss in tobacco trade. Since then, he buys lottery tickets regularly, wears a bunch of amulets and whenever he hears of a sadhu, prostrates before him.

Seeing Santulal, Motilal gestures with his hand and whispers, 'Don't talk now. Baba is partaking of some refreshment And beware, he has a habit of throwing whatever is within easy reach. Better come under my umbrella.'

Sitting in the shelter of Motilal's umbrella, Santu cannot blink as he observes the sadhu eating. Although he could not be too sure in the fading light, it looked as if the man was chewing a big leg.

Motilal gave him a nudge, 'What are you gaping for? I couldn't believe my eyes either!'

Santu moved closer to Motilal, 'What did you see?'

Motilal said under his breath, 'I didn't see the whole thing. I came here when the sun was going down. A fox was gasping in front of Baba, dying. It was bleeding from the mouth and its ribcage was still moving. Baba lit a pyre and thrust the living animal in. Upon God, I swear in the name of Ma Kali. And as you can see, he is eating it with such relish!'

Santulal has tasted pig's meat, but has not managed to eat fox's. Hearing this, he sidles closer to Motilal. Motilal whispers into his ear, 'An incarnation of Mahadeva, he has the spirits under his thumb. Do you understand? It's a great fortune to come in contact with such a man.'

After eating the fox, the sadhu wiped his hand on the grass and stretched himself on the ground. Motilal went forward cautiously and started massaging his legs.

Santulal had found it nauseating to watch the sadhu eating a fox. When Motilal signalled, he crawled up close, touched the ground near the sadhu's feet with his head and started cribbing, 'Baba! I am a great sinner. But you would understand, baba, an unhappy man like me cannot survive without committing a few sins! That's why I've been thinking, if I get your blessings, I will become a good man from tomorrow.'

The sadhu was lying on his back. Hearing Santu, he turned his head and stared at him for a moment. His eyes were sharp. Santu felt as though he had been pricked by a needle.

The sadhu, however, did not bad-mouth him. He said with a smile, 'Ungrateful bastard! Tomorrow, come back with a hibiscus flower and five rupees. Now, get lost.'

Looking around, Santu retched as he saw the fox's intestine, skin and the half-burnt head, and left the place. He didn't go back again. He had no face to do so. A hibiscus was fine, but where was he to get five rupees from?

The sadhu had left, saying he wanted to take a holy dip on the Chaitra Sankranti, but has left behind dark patches on the grass that look like ringworm. A faint rotten smell still lingers. Santulal has heard one becomes mad if one eats fox meat.

Being unsure if he would manage to light the bidi in the wind, for sometime, Santu debates if he should strike the half matchstick on the rib of the matchbox. Ultimately, he comes down a few steps from the top, to where the wind was partially blocked by the mound. Saying, 'Jai Ma Kali!' he strikes the match. It is gone ... gone ... oh god! He puts the bidi between his cupped hands and takes a drag at it as if his life depended on it.

Ma Kali is great! The bidi has been lit. The matchstick had in fact blown itself out, but Santulal had managed to light the bidi while the tip of the stick was still glowing.

A happy Santu sits down on the mound and looks at the horizon. When this bidi is finished, he would light another from its light before resuming his journey.

Nothing much could be done about his sins. He could not confess to anyone. Perhaps the sadhu took away Motilal's sins before leaving. As he sits there smoking, Santulal says to himself: No! From tomorrow, I am going to become an honest fellow.

Seeing a bus coming along the main road, he gets up quickly and hurries towards it.

The bus stops too, as he waves. But the conductor, Nityacharan, knows him personally. He blocks the doorway with his arm saying, 'Do you have the money for the fare?'

'Yes, of course.'

After some hesitation, Nityacharan lets Santu in, but insults him needlessly. Says he, 'Don't take a seat. Sit on the floor.'

But that is to Santulal's advantage. He would be less conspicuous on the floor. He may even save on the fare. Besides, there were no vacant seats. As soon as he sits down, he takes out a bidi from his pocket and offers it to Nityacharan. Things would be easier if he accepted; otherwise, he would make life difficult for Santulal.

Nityacharan accepts the bidi. He had to. His second wife has written to him from Ulubere. Standing at the door, despite the rushing wind, he manages to light the bidi as if by sleight of hand. Then he takes out a soggy postcard from his chest pocket and starts reading the running hand intently. Anger, irritation, detachment and happiness play upon his face intermittently. Chameli has written:

> I touch the lotus feet a thousand times. Thereafter, I must inform that the areca nuts have been plucked. But my elder and younger brothers-in-law have not provided me with an account. They have given only a small amount to me. Please insist on a detailed account when you come home next month. They harass me no end. Why? Am I nobody in the family? Even the stepson calls me 'Tinni's mother', not ma. I have so many things to tell you. They say both wives should get equal shares. Big deal! I have sold my share of straws to Shyamlal. I still have five rupees left out of that. Your money order is yet to reach. Tell me how can I manage the expenses. No one bothers to ask me how much I had to spend when Tinni was down with dysentery. Who do I have? On market day, I gave some cash to brother-in-law Mukunda for purchasing talcum powder. Was it a sin? I gave it to him because he was going to the market. He did not even return the money to me. He returned it to Tinni and said, 'There is no need to deck out like a queen. People say all sorts of things.' Your first wife goes around slandering my character. I can vouch in the name of Ma Kali that there is no truth in it. There is no more space in the postcard. Lord of my heart, please keep me at your lotus feet for all times. Yours, Chameli.

The last sentence was a straight lift from the play 'Ravana's Death'. Heaving a sigh, Nityacharan puts the postcard back in his pocket. The bidi has died down. He lights it again.

Santulal has been observing Nityacharan's expressions keenly. He has to travel a distance of only a mile or so. He has to somehow spend the time. He wished the letter was longer; he wondered why people wrote such short missives.

In the end, Nityacharan waived the fare. While Santu was getting down, he merely commented, 'Hey Four-twenty! Does this bus run on water? Doesn't petrol cost money?'

Santu couldn't care less whether the bus ran on petrol or water. What he runs on is still a mystery to him. And he has managed to pull along for all these fifty years or thereabouts.

He was lucky he did not have to walk the distance in this heat. The bus ride was a bonus.

For some time, he had stopped talking to Sukhchandra. But no longer. He has decided, it was not Sukhchandra's fault. After all, he did not woo Saraswati, she herself fell for him. In fact, it was better that she was with Sukhchandra instead of someone else. The man does not hurt people unnecessarily. He is light hearted and easygoing. He lives well, blows up whatever he earns. He would buy the best things available in the market. During the season, he would buy mangos or jackfruits even if they were costly. He even has a radio in his house. He doesn't treat his first wife Shefali – who is barren – badly either. He has left his old house for her and has constructed a new one for Saraswati. He lives in both places.

After much deliberation, Santulal has reached the conclusion that it was not a bad thing to happen. Of course, in the beginning, he used to feel hurt. But it was a fact that with three kids, Saraswati was a noose around his neck. For example, last night, he watched a play at Kharubere, then, after it was over at the crack of dawn, he had a thoroughly enjoyable nap, and is now leisurely going back when half the day is over. Had Saraswati

---

Four-twenty: Section 420 of the Indian Penal Code dealing with cheating. Commonly used to refer to petty cheats, conmen.

been with him, this would have been unthinkable. Since that female left, he has been a free man. Moreover, the kids get to eat regularly and have clothes on them. It was difficult to make out how Saraswati actually looked like after six years with Santulal. But nowadays, she has sloughed off her old skin and wears a new one. Her arms and legs are fuller, she looks sexy. Her eyes flash. She is fine.

Santulal used to go around with a long face. One day, Sukhchandra called him and said, 'Brother Santu, God exists in you and He exists in me. Are we different? Saraswati came and parked herself here, how could I throw her out?'

After talking like this for some time, Sukhchandra had won over Santu. But Saraswati still bears old grudges. She turns her face away if she meets Santulal and talks ill about him in a loud voice, addressing the sky and the wind.

And one can talk ill about Santulal for centuries. The story of his life is a litany of petty thefts and cheating. Those stories are old. Last week, when Santu saw his little daughter Kunti playing hopscotch at Palpara, he stopped in his tracks as a sudden surge of fatherly affection drowned his mind. After all, she was his offspring. The girl too, after finishing her turn, ran towards him. She gave him a broad smile and called, 'Baba!' What solace it was! The girl was wearing colourful underpants, but had nothing above her waist.

Santu's eyes are habitual sinners. His sinful gaze would invariably spot tempting objects. As he looked at his daughter, he noticed, a part of the waistband of her underpants was turned inside-out. And nestling in that fold – clearly – were a fifty-paisa coin and some smaller change.

Santu embraced his daughter and kissed her. The girl then returned to her hopscotch court and Santu went towards the market to buy cigarettes for his master. And on the way, he realised, somehow some coins – one fifty-paisa, two ten-paisa and one five-paisa – had found their way into his hands. It was true! He could swear in the name of any god, he just didn't notice how the coins came to be in his palm. He just didn't know!

But since they had come, Santu considered them a gift from god and repaid His generosity by quickly drinking hooch before returning. At the main gate leading to his master's house, Saraswati was waiting, Kunti tagging on to her. There was no escape. The girl spotted him first and shouted, 'There ma! There he comes!' And Saraswati instantaneously turned on an old gramophone record, 'Bastard, son of a fallen woman, shit of a mangy dog! There'd be no one to cremate you when you die. Wretched fellow! I gave the girl money for buying lentil, and the girl is stupid too, why on earth did she have to flaunt her affection to that son of a cow-stealer? And see what sense this corpse has! He stole money from his own daughter, from the waistband of her underpants! Tell me, you lecher, what can you not do for money?'

She would have continued. But the master's wife came out and said sharply, 'Saraswati! I'll throw you out if you shout in such filthy language. And Santu! Get lost this very moment! One is a thief and the other has a mouth like a drain! My child will hear all this and pick up bad words! Get lost.'

Saraswati is not scared of the babu's wife. She often bares her fangs. But that day, she did not go any further. She only threatened to get Santu thrashed by Bishu of the wheat mill.

That very evening, Bishu dragged Santulal behind their shop and landed a few blows. He would have inflicted more damage, but Sukhchandra heard the commotion and came out. He said, 'Forget it, it was only seventy-five paise.' But although Sukhchandra forgives him, Saraswati doesn't. Arms akimbo, she comes out, stands before Santu and says, 'He'll be free only after he bleeds from his mouth!' Santulal falls at Saraswati's feet and pleads, 'It will never happen again.'

To this day, Santulal asks himself, did he actually pinch the coins? And replies, with a shiver, 'No! I can swear in the name of

Ma Kali. Why don't you understand? The bloody coins were crooks. They jumped into my hand when I was unmindful, just to spite me!'

Santulal wants to share these melancholy tales with someone. He wants to unburden himself completely. But the sadhu has disappeared. And who else can he trust?

Yesterday, in the evening, the master's wife gave him money to buy river fish. She repeatedly told him, 'Santu, return the change, don't run away.'

Santulal made a promise to himself: Enough is enough! I ought to become a decent person. I should be able to hold my head high.

He would have returned the change had he himself returned. As usual, it was his fate. There were no river fish in the market. There were some small fishes like nata and chang, which the babus wouldn't eat. He was actually returning home with the money. And then, Haragobinda told him there was a jatra at Kharubere; would Santulal accompany him? Santulal was not one to consider the pros and cons. It was a moonlit night and a pleasant breeze was blowing. He did not feel like going back to his master's house. He thought – let me indulge in sin for this one last time. From tomorrow, yes from tomorrow, in god's name, I'll turn into a good fellow. So thinking, he drank hooch to his heart's content. Then they hit the road towards Kharubere.

Therefore, presently, he finds it a little embarrassing to return. If he went to babu's house straightaway, babu's wife would give him hell.

So, Santulal goes over to Sukhchandra's wheat grinder in the market. 'How's life, Sukhchandra? Is everything fine?'

A decent chap, Sukhchandra has a casual look about him. Come hell or high weather, he never looks grim. He says, 'How can things be fine? You vanished from the scene yesterday, didn't you? There's a big commotion in your master's house. Go there.'

'I am going there,' says Santulal and sits down on a bench. Bishu was running the electric grinder. A cloud of fine wheat flour was hanging in the air. He says irritably, 'Better leave now. Don't disturb us when we are busy.'

Santulal snarls at him, 'Who the hell are you? The owner of the store says nothing; why do *you* butt in?'

It looked like the beginning of a blazing row, but at that moment, Santu's son came into the shop and said to Sukhchandra, 'Baba, ma has asked you to take home some vegetables.'

Santu observes the child full of affection. His son, yes, his son, calling Sukhchandra 'Baba'. Aha, let him. Doesn't he need someone to call baba? Santulal admits, he himself doesn't deserve the honour.

As his son leaves the shop, Santu follows. After a few paces, the boy turns around and says, 'Why are you following me?'

Santu retorts, 'Does this road belong to your father?'

'You better go elsewhere, otherwise I'll tell ma.'

'What will you tell?'

'You stole money from Kunti. Don't you remember?'

'Oh! I stole! That useless girl lost the coins when she was playing hopscotch, and blames me!'

'Even then, you shouldn't come too close.'

'You forgot your father, Bistu?'

The boy goes away.

Near the pond in Palpara, Sukhchandra's first wife, Shefali accosts Santulal. She was returning after a bath in the pond. She tells Santulal, 'I have to talk to you.'

Shefali is fat. Her body has become flaccid and she has a sheet of prickly heat rashes over her skin. Her podgy rotund face reminds one of a katla fish. She has the habit of chewing tobacco.

She says with a smile, 'Have you heard the news? You're going to be a father again!'

But one cannot become a father just like that. Santu says with surprise, 'How can I become a father again?'

'It's the same thing. Your wife is going to be a mother!'

Santu says with a bashful smile, 'You say all sorts of things, bouthan!'

'Take it from me. But let me also tell you, if the baby in Saraswati's womb is not yours, it is not Sukhchandra's either!'

On hearing the news, Santulal feels happy about Saraswati. Aha! Let her have more children. She is fond of children. She forgets everything when she is with her offspring.

A happy Santulal says, 'Good, very good.'

'Good? What's good about it? Whatever people might say, I know Sukhchandra's capacity. That weakling can never father a child. If he could, people wouldn't call me barren. You think Sukh babu has done it? You are a simpleton. There's a twist in the tale!'

'A twist in the tale?'

A sly smile spreads over Shefali's podgy face. She says, 'Don't you have eyes? Don't you understand why Bishu thrashed you the other day? Don't you know why he refused to take up a better job that Dinabandhu babu had offered him ? Don't you know why he is hanging on to this place despite a paltry salary of twenty rupees plus food? Don't you understand anything? Haven't you noticed how close Bishu and Saraswati are? Keep your eyes and ears open. Then others won't have to tell you. Now, go home and think about all this with a cool head.'

Santulal does not understand what is there to be thought about. It is clear as daylight. But the fact is that he no longer bothers about these things. The main thing is: Saraswati is going to have another baby.

As he enters the compound, he meets babu first. Babu is in the garden, lying in an easy chair, reading a book. He is always reading books. Santu has heard, babu is a famous teacher in some college. He knows much about many things, although he cannot make out if a husk of paddy has a seed in it. Anyway, it is better that he can't make out many such things. Life would have been more difficult for Santulal if he did.

Looking up, babu says, 'Oh! Santulal! Where had you been?'

'I am sorry, babu! It won't happen again.'

'I know that. But people were worried about you.'

'It won't happen again.'

Babu is lightly built. He does not talk much. He only says with a touch of remorse, 'It is getting so difficult to find trustworthy men.'

There is a pall of gloom in the inner quarters. Boudi has just got up after her afternoon siesta. Face swollen, she looks rather like a minor demon. On top of that, betel juice has dried up in the corners of her lips, like congealed blood. There are beads of sweat on her forehead and neck. She is walking to the well, the end of her sari trailing behind her along the ground. Seeing Santulal in the veranda of the inner quarters, she stops, 'Who allowed you to come in? Get out!'

Santulal quickly holds his ears, 'It won't happen again!'

The spirit is usually at a low ebb when someone has just got up from sleep. Boudi too has been feeling a little listless. She says with a yawn, 'Have you brought the money?'

'Please recover it from my salary.'

'Go and make tea.'

Santulal is not the person designated for making tea. He works outdoors. He lifts water from the well, tends the cows, milks them, looks after the garden, washes clothes and runs errands. Saraswati does the household chores: cooking, washing utensils, mopping floors. So Santulal is a little surprised when boudi asks him to make tea.

He is not sure how to go about it, but slowly makes his way in. At the entrance to the kitchen, Saraswati has been lying down on the end of her sari, fast asleep.

Let her sleep, poor thing! After all, she's going to be a mother again. At times like this, a woman often feels drained out. A fly was buzzing around the open mouth of Saraswati. Santulal drives it away with a wave of his hand.

He enters the kitchen gingerly, stepping over his former wife. He cannot get the better of the kerosene stove, but plays with it for some time. Hearing the noise, Saraswati turns around and, fixing him with a burning gaze, says, 'What's this? Why have you entered the kitchen with unclean feet? And your clothes are dirty too. Are you a human being? Your clothes haven't been washed for days and you have even been shitting wearing them! God knows in which dump you spent last night! Get lost!'

Santulal gives her a broad smile. She looks fine. A woman looks different when she is about to be a mother.

As she gets up, she says, 'How did you cross the threshold? Did you step over me?'

'What could I do?'

'What do you mean – what could I do? Should you step over a living being?'

Santulal says in a sombre voice, 'You are pregnant, why do you lie down in all sorts of places? You ought to be more cautious now.'

For some reason, Saraswati turns silent on hearing this. Without another word, she goes out somewhere, perhaps to wash. A little later, she returns – her face wet – and says, 'Step aside, I'll make the tea.'

Santulal steps aside, but doesn't leave. He keeps looking at Saraswati intently, leaning on the doorjamb. She is aware that he has been watching her, but doesn't turn around.

She doesn't turn around not because she is scared of Santulal. Actually, she doesn't want to show her wretched face to anyone.

The wicks had burnt off in the stove. Saraswati takes out the casing and pulls the wicks up before lighting the stove. After putting the kettle on fire, she goes out to wash the kerosene off her hands, leaving the matchbox on the floor.

Santulal doesn't have a matchbox. He lit a bidi a long time ago with his last, broken matchstick. For him, considering the pros and cons is a big hassle. He makes off after picking up the matchbox. He has plenty of things to do. He has to lift water, feed the cows and smoke the cowshed to drive away mosquitoes. And before that, he has to find a cosy nook to smoke a bidi.

Sitting under the shade of a tamarind tree, Santulal observes the splendour of colours in the western sky. He feels refreshed when he smokes a bidi. He tends to be at peace with the world. He feels even more refreshed when he drinks hooch made of palm sap. And while smoking cannabis, he is simply transported to heaven.

When his bidi is almost over, the six-year-old daughter of the master, Babli, runs in from somewhere, hangs on to his shoulders and says, 'Santuda, did you steal money and run away?'

Santu beams at her and says, 'No, honestly, I didn't.'

'I know. Yesterday, you stole cash and ran away. Hold your ears.'

Santu holds his ears, sticks out his tongue and says, 'Shame on me! What I've done is awful. It won't happen again.'

Babli has been learning new tricks every day. She goes to school these days. She learns so many things there. Like now. She picks up a twig and tells Santulal, 'Stretch your hands!'

He obliges. Babli hits him with the twig held in her slender hand. She says, 'Will you do it again?'

'No, never.'

'Kneel down.'

Santu kneels down.

The little girl cannot decide what more can be done with her captive. She says, 'That should be fine. I have punished you, haven't I? I must hug you now.' So saying, she holds Santulal's head over her shoulder and runs her fingers through his hair. She says, 'Tut, tut, tut! Did I hurt you, Santuda?'

Santu feels a pang of remorse. An ocean of tears wells up in his eyes. He shakes his head and says, 'No, no, it didn't hurt. I am a thief, ma. Even my children hate me. Please hit me every day. Will you?'

'Oh yes! I'll give you such terrible punishments! But don't be scared, I'll also hug you.'

There is some commotion in the kitchen about the missing matchbox. Let there be. Santulal cannot be bothered by small things. His hands are full. He gets up and goes to the cowshed.

In the evening, when he goes to the garden to remove babu's easy chair and the small stool on which tumblers and teacups are kept, he finds a pack of cigarettes. There are two whole cigarettes still left. Santu thinks, if he took them, people would call him a thief. But could this pack be lying here within easy reach if it had not been god's will?

Santu hides the pack in a kamini bush nearby. He would enjoy smoking the cigarettes at night, after supper.

Saraswati has left after finishing her chores. She did not make a big issue about the missing matchbox. Although he happened to cross her path, she did not even glare at him. Babu and his wife too have gone to bed early tonight.

Lying down on a hemp mat in a veranda outside the house, Santulal is smoking a cigarette. Saraswati comes out of the darkness and says, 'Who told you I was pregnant?'

Santu swings his legs with a flourish and says, 'You became pregnant thrice when you were with me, I know the signs. I don't need to be told.'

Saraswati sits down on her haunches and says, 'Don't lie. Shefali has been spreading tales. She must've told you. Bitch! She can't get pregnant, and if someone else does, finds faults. Do you think Sukhchandra would keep me if such things became public?'

Santulal scratches his head.

Saraswati says in a small voice, 'Listen carefully. Please tell Sukhchandra that I was up to no mischief when I was with you and neither do I do any such thing now. Do you follow? He would value your words. Sukhchandra is with that bitch today, and she is sure to poison his mind through the night. That man will turn against me. You must meet Sukhchandra tomorrow and tell him this, as you discuss other things.'

Santulal says absently, 'All right, I'll tell him.'

'Please do. I know, you are not a bad person. Keep these two rupees.' Saying so, Saraswati starts untying the knot at the end of her sari to take out some coins.

Santulal finds it terribly embarrassing. He says hurriedly, 'No, no, please don't bother.'

'Please take this. You get a salary of ten rupees a month. It hardly covers your expenses. Keep this. I've left the door open; must go back soon.'

'Yes, you better go. Take care, there are plenty of petty thieves around.'

'That's true.' So saying, Saraswati vanishes into the darkness.

Santulal lights the second cigarette. Saraswati said he is a good person. She could not have been serious! She just wanted to please him. Had he been a good person, everyone would have recognised him as one.

Santulal looks at the cigarette in his hand for a long moment. He gets angry with himself. Suddenly, he throws away the nearly full-length cigarette and slaps himself on his cheeks several times.

But that does not lessen his anger. He pulls himself by the scruff of his neck. Throws himself out of the main gate saying, 'Get lost you son-of-a-sow, stupid wretched thief! If you show your face again, I'll thrash you with my shoes.'

Saying this, Santulal shakes the dust off his hands and returns. Tomorrow itself, he would go and talk to Sukhchandra and convince him that Saraswati is a faithful partner. The baby in her womb is Sukhchandra's. And he would also return the two rupees to Saraswati. He must not accept bribe. That old Santulal is dead.

For a while, Santulal sits motionless, inundated by happiness. He feels like a large-hearted man; a pleasant breeze blows through his chest. It feels great.

Smoke is still swirling up from the cigarette, from under a bush. Quite a bit of it still remains. A meaningless waste.

Santulal goes and picks up the cigarette. He starts puffing it merrily. He shakes the matchbox; plenty of matchsticks left. In his left pocket are the two rupees given by Saraswati.

Santulal thinks: this is my last act of sin. Come tomorrow, I promise, I'm going to be a different person.